All's Fairy in Love and Murder

All's Fairy in Love and Murder

K.M. Waller

ABOUT THE BOOK

Be careful what you wish for!

Juniper is a fairy princess living in a fairy godparent world. But like most fairy tales–she wants to be where the people are…

Determined to prove she can handle humans like the rest of the fairy godparent population, she sneaks out of her protected magical home to sprinkle fairy dust and give a downtrodden man some luck. But she's a misguided fairy and everything quickly goes awry.

When her interference leads to a murder, she has no choice but to find his killer and bring them to justice. But solving a crime after losing her magic wand and with very little fairy dust proves challenging.

Is Juniper ready to take on the human world and all the complications that come with catching a murderer?

Dedication

To Nadine. May the fairies bless you as you have blessed me!

ACKNOWLEDGMENTS

I would like to thank my first readers and friends, Becky and Gisele. You two ladies are always there for me when I need you. Along with them, I couldn't do this without the support and patience of my family. Thank you for supporting me through my crazy moods and forgiving me for feeding you frozen waffles for dinner when I'm close to missing a deadline. xoxo

Chapter One

"Fairy, fairy, quite contrary, how does your boredom grow?" I stared at my reflection in the courtyard fountain's translucent water while plucking plum-colored petals from an orchid's long stem. I dropped them into the fountain and watched as they floated out of reach to the other side. If I sprinkled some fairy dust in the water, I'd be able to observe into the human world, but I'd grown weary of having only a bird's eye view.

"You are outrageously melodramatic, Juniper." My best friend and fellow fairy, Iris, sat on the edge of the fountain and crossed her ankles. The ends of her wings dipped into the water. She lifted her face toward the sun, exposing her pale, slender neck.

A palace guard stumbled over his feet as he passed by. He caught himself before spilling to the ground and his cheeks turned a rosy shade of red. I understood his clumsiness around her. Iris was the second most beautiful fairy in our land. My mom, Queen Poppy, being the first.

I waited for the guard to disappear down the corridor before lowering my voice to a near whisper. "Are we on for tonight?"

Iris grumbled a few unintelligible words under her breath and the tips of her wings flickered to highlight her agitation. She reached into her dress pocket and retrieved the parchment. She placed it on the edge of the fountain. "You are the biggest cliché. The sheltered princess has everything she could possibly desire but wants to slum it with the humans instead."

I tossed the orchid stem at her and picked up the missive, glancing around again to make sure we weren't being watched. "Be judge-y later. What's the fairy errand?" I unfolded the paper and read the name and address. *John Bleaker, 325 Palmer Road, Lilac Cove.*

"The human male needs a sprinkle of fairy luck to help with an interview tomorrow. This is the closest FE I could snag. He's a boring man who lives only a few miles away in a boring little town on Florida's gulf coast. Lives by himself and is in bed most nights by nine p.m. It's a simple in-and-out job." She grasped my wrist and gave it a gentle squeeze. "If we get caught, your parents will feed me to the trolls. Or worse, they won't let me live in the palace anymore."

"Now who's being dramatic? We won't get caught," I assured her, but she only fluttered her eyelashes in an exaggerated eye roll and fluffed the blonde curls that circled her head like a golden halo.

I'd been planning my one-night excursion into the human world for more than a year, ever since my twenty-fifth birthday, when I should have been allowed to join my fellow fairies as a fairy godparent. I'd trained alongside all the other fairies and, at the last minute, my parents had pulled the palace rug out from under me.

Being a godmother was my birthright, after all.

I took in the lush, green courtyard and the pristine gray bricks of the palace walls. Being the only heir to the North American fairy throne happened to be my birthright, too. According to my parents, that took precedence. Not to mention that a couple of fairies had left our world to live in the human world over the past couple of years and that made the entire kingdom nervous. There were only so many of us left.

For twenty-six years I'd been trapped inside the protective magical dome of our home in the swamps of Juniper Springs, Florida. That's right, I'm named after our fairy land.

Every other fairy took on the responsibility of godparent on their twenty-fifth year. They then ventured out to wave their wands and sprinkle enchanted dust to help the humans. We called them fairy errands or FEs. With so much evil in the world, humans needed every sprinkle we could give them. That's what I needed to be doing, too.

Instead, I had to spend my days preparing to ascend to the throne.

Don't get me wrong. Living with the humans on a permanent basis didn't hold any appeal so my parents fears were unfounded. And fairies who chose that path didn't get the option to come back. Just ask my Aunt Mossandra, who I've never actually met and have only seen in a portrait hanging on the palace wall.

But day after day of palace duties like arranging nobility banquets and settling fairy disputes and this gal needed a little break in the routine. An adventure.

My only two connections to the world where everyone else traveled was the courtyard fountain and the human-written books Iris smuggled back from her assignments.

The king's distinct voice boomed from somewhere inside the main halls.

"Uh oh. King Hypnum sounds mad. Again. I'm out." Iris stood and shook the water off of her wings. She stretched out her arms and allowed a pout to pull down the edges of her glossy pink lips. "I'm losing my shimmer and am in desperate need of a glitter bath." She pulled me to my feet and placed light kisses on both of my cheeks. "There's still plenty of time to change your mind about tonight."

I tilted my head to the side and held her violet gaze. "You know I won't."

Her shoulders sagged. "That's what worries me most—your inability to let go of something once you've set your mind to it." She fluttered her wings and lifted a few inches from the ground. She glided to the nearest exit but picked up her pace once my father came around the corner, his always present entourage close behind.

"When I find out who's been skimming, they'll spend their eternity with a wad of thorns stuck up their…" He caught sight of me and stopped short.

I waved the tips of my fingers at him. "Don't stop on my account, Daddy. Where will the thorns be going?"

He pursed his lips and met me at the fountain. "Hello, dearest. I didn't see you there." He gave the top of my head a quick peck. Between my parents, I mostly resembled my dad, with his dark brown hair and gray eyes with a sharp, pointy nose settled in between.

I warmed under his affection, almost feeling guilty for my devious plans later on that evening. Almost.

"Who's skimming what?" I asked.

Irritation returned to his expression. "The enchantment dust harvesters are reporting stolen crop."

"We'll find the culprits, your majesty," Amaranth, the captain of the royal guard and my on-again, off-again boyfriend, assured the king.

Amaranth and I avoided eye contact with each other as at this moment we happened to be in the off-again territory. He'd caught me outside the palace walls with a copy of the works of Edgar Allen Poe. Long story short, we'd argued about what he'd called my "infatuation with the human world." The nerve. Just because something interested me didn't mean I'd become infatuated with it.

Dad must have noticed the tension between us because he cleared his throat a few times before gesturing toward the main hall. "Your mother awaits me in the throne room, so we'll be on our way. You have your itinerary for the remainder of the day, I assume. Will you be dining with us this evening?"

I turned on my sweetest, daughterly smile but

my pulse quickened. "Iris and I have plans tonight. Tomorrow?"

"I look forward to it." He led his private guards and the other palace lackeys out of the courtyard.

I blew out a hard breath and waited for my heart to return to its normal pace. My wings twitched, and I flicked them to work out the tension. At least I'd been able to avoid my mom all day. She could take one look at me and know when I was up to something—like a sixth sense.

I glanced at the sun and estimated that I had four hours before I set my plan into motion. Just enough time to immerse myself in my newest book. The itinerary my father spoke of, which included picking flower arrangements for the main hall's dining tables, could wait.

I snapped my fingers, making my wand appear in the palm of my other hand, and then withdrew the miniaturized version of *Pride & Prejudice* from my pocket. I tapped it three times and said, "Big." The book grew to normal size and I clutched it against my chest.

If the person I planned to visit tonight was half as interesting as Elizabeth Bennet or Fitzwilliam Darcy, I was in for quite the treat.

Chapter Two

A succession of knocks in a rhythmic pattern sounded from the other side of my door shortly after sundown. I cracked it open and found Iris on the other side, dressed in a hooded cloak.

"What's with the weird knocking?" I asked.

"It's a secret knock so you'll know it's me." She pushed through the door, a dress laid over her arm and a bag in her hand.

I closed it behind her and turned the lock. "It wouldn't have mattered who knocked, I still would have opened it."

Her expression warred between a smile and frown. "I don't think this is a good idea."

I took the shimmering dress from her and worked it over my body. A little tight, thanks to my curves and Iris's lack of. I regarded myself in the full-length mirror. "Why? Because I don't get the point of the secret knock?"

She took my hand and pulled me around to face her. "I love you lots. Like the sister I never had."

"You have a sister. Her name is Marigold, remember?"

She looked up at the ceiling like I'd just made her point for her. "Don't take this the wrong way, but you're a bit naïve about the way the human world works. It's not your fault. It's your sheltered palace life that's to blame."

I yanked my hand back and placed it on my hip. "You've been going to the human world for only a year, and you live in the palace too. I'll be as world-wise as you before morning."

She perched on the edge of my bed, staring off at something distant out the window. "But I've seen things. So many things. They're seared in here forever," she said, tapping the side of her head.

I dug my toes into the plush carpet. "I want to see things, too. Searing or not. And if you really loved me, you'd stop trying to change my mind and help me finish getting dressed."

Her eyebrows drew together sharply. "Manipulative. Nice. You might do well in the human world after all." She opened her sack and pulled out a yellow mop that reminded me of a dead animal covered with pollen.

"What's that?" I asked.

"Your wig. We have to change your appearance to look more like me. While my wand will get you past the gates, the guards still know you, and a lot of them know me too, if you know what I mean." She winked and made a kissy face.

Despite her claim of my naivety, I knew exactly what she meant. Iris was a shameless flirt.

Our wands were our main source of identification, each fairy having a particular wand fashioned from a juniper tree and blessed by the king and queen. "I've planned for that. I know the guard schedule tonight. It's a newbie. I'm almost positive we've yet to cross paths."

"Still, wear the wig, just in case." She twisted and piled my dark hair onto my head and jammed the wig on top, securing it with a few bobby pins. "There. Now for your face."

I poked at the thing on my head. "I have to change my face, too?"

"I wouldn't be caught dead without a healthy layer of glitter. Since you're technically going to be me, you should play the part." She nudged me to sit in front of my vanity. "Close your eyes."

I did as she instructed and felt a pouf bounce across my face. I sneezed after some powder went up my nose.

"Okay, open," she said, and stood back. "Perfection."

I opened my eyes to a reflection of true ridiculousness. Purple, pink, and silver glitter covered every inch of skin on my face. I shifted the wig. Good thing I'd be able to hide most of it beneath the cloak's hood.

Iris clapped her hands. "This might actually work."

"Of course it will." I'd waited a year for this perfectly-planned night. Rarely was the palace without guests, but tonight it was only the royal family.

A chime from the main village sounded three times, alerting the fairies that is was time for them to attend to their godparent duties. The main guard would turn an hourglass and for fifteen minutes an exit would form in the protective dome. After the sands finished sifting through, the exit would close until they turned it over again at daybreak. No one else out and nothing could get in.

I lifted off of the ground, the excitement pushing my wings to beat faster.

Iris removed her cloak and arranged it around my wings and shoulders. She pulled the hood over my head, and I could see her hands shake.

I kissed her on each cheek. "I'll be back by daybreak, and we'll laugh over all the wonderful and amazing things I've seen."

She bit her bottom lip, but nodded and opened my door.

I stepped into the hallway checking for voices. "All clear."

As soon as I vacated the doorway, the door shut hard behind me and I heard the lock click into place. I lifted off the ground and navigated to and through the palace kitchen. The kitchen workers bustled around and nobody so much as glanced in my direction. With a rush of adrenaline, I whooshed out the back door and floated down to the village.

Fairy men and women formed a line at the main exit. The dome shielded us from human eyes, as well as other magical beings that would like to see fairies become extinct.

I kept my gaze trained on the ground and when my turn came up for my bag of enchantment dust, I lowered my voice. "Nice evening, huh?"

"I guess," the gate guard answered.

I presented my wand and as he handed over my bag, a familiar voice caught my attention.

"I'll take over here, soldier. Why don't you take a break?"

Amaranth.

I snatched my bag out of the guard's hands. "See ya."

"Wait," Amaranth called after me.

I stopped, not wanting to cause a chase scene. I pulled the hood down further around my face and waited for him to approach me.

"Juniper?" He leaned down into my face while lifting the top of the hood. "What are you doing?"

"Shh." I pulled him to the side and glanced at his face for the first time since our argument. It was a face I'd seen almost daily since we were six years old. As handsome as any fairy male could be, his chestnut hair and matching eyes were features I'd memorized long ago. "How did you know it was me?"

He lifted an eyebrow. "The birthmark near your elbow."

Ah. Apparently he'd memorized some of my features too. The birthmark must have shown when I reached for the bag. My own impatience had done me in.

His gaze took in my moppish wig and glitter disguise. "Please tell me you aren't sneaking out to the human world."

I smiled and tugged the hood back into place. "Okay, I won't tell you."

He squared his shoulders. There were many great qualities about Amaranth, the top being he took his job as captain of the guard seriously. "I can't let you go."

My smile died along with my excitement. I'd been so close. "You can. You don't want to."

He crossed his arms.

I grabbed his forearm. "Please do this for me. I'll be back before anyone else knows I'm gone."

The newbie called to us from his position near the stacked bags of dust. "Hey Captain, the gate is closing in a minute. Is she going through or not?"

"She's not." He shook off my hand. "It's for your own safety, Princess."

My chest tightened. Why didn't he understand?

The sands poured through the hourglass faster by the second. I gripped my wand tight and turned as if walking back toward the palace with him.

Then I did something I haven't done since we were kids. I lifted into the air and shoved him hard enough to knock him down. "I'm sorry, but I am going."

Before Amaranth could scramble to his feet, I zipped through the portal and turned to watch as it closed behind me. Anger had lit up his face, but I'd deal with that and his disappointment in me later.

If I didn't have my adventure tonight, I'd never have another chance.

Chapter Three

My heart *thwapped, thwapped, thwapped* hard in my chest. I hovered above ground on the opposite side of my fairy homeland. The portal didn't reopen, and no one else had followed me through.

I wanted to see and touch everything, but first things first. I tapped my head with Iris's wand and said, "Small."

I shrank to the size of a bird and fluttered to the tops of the trees. Even though I wasn't allowed to godparent, I'd watched the training of my fellow fairies enough to know how to hide from humans and other creepy things prowling the swamp at night.

I whisked off the cloak and hung it on a nearby branch. My borrowed dress shimmered in the moonlight, and I stuck my enchantment dust in the pocket.

I inhaled deeply, but immediately wrinkled my nose. Freedom smelled awful swampy, and a little like animal waste. The sounds were much different on this side of the dome, too. The frogs croaked louder, and in the distance, I could hear vehicle engines and the blasting sound of a train's horn. While I'd never seen these human things up close, I'd read about them and heard the stories brought back from the other fairies. I twirled in a circle and squealed. Now I had the chance to experience them firsthand. How would one night be enough?

Again, I tapped the wand on my head. "To John Bleaker's, 325 Palmer Road, Lilac Cove." With a whizz and a poof and a blink, I appeared inside a human dwelling. "Big," I said and tapped my head again to return to normal size. I furled my wings so I didn't bump into anything inside the house.

If I finished my FE quickly enough then I could take the long way home. Unless Amaranth ran straight to my dad. In that case, I'd better hurry.

The home I'd poofed into smelled of fresh cut flowers, and I located a vase on a coffee table filled with bright yellow roses. The color of friendship. Once I'd sat at the fountain and watched a woman who watched hours and hours of a television channel called HGTV. Only through this did I know that John Bleaker decorated in a coastal theme with different shades of blues in the furniture and the pictures on the walls. Beside the flowers sat another vase filled with an assortment of shells.

I took the largest off the top and put it to my ear. I'd never been to the ocean, but I'd heard from other fairies that the sharp windy-whooshes were the same sounds the waves made as they broke against the shore.

Along the wall behind a couch were three bookshelves filled with an array of hardback books. Each row of books was held upright by a painted brick bookend. Miniature sailboats were painted on each brick. I ran my fingers along the spines of the books. So many interesting titles. If I had enough time, I'd snag one on the way out. I'd have to ask Iris to return it at a later date.

At the end of the bookshelves hung what looked to be a large rectangular bird cage. When I peered inside, a little chittering face pushed out from beneath wood shavings.

"Hello, there," I said and pulled out my wand. I tapped the top of the squirrel's head and said, "Speak."

"A real-life fairy. I'll be," he whispered, the amazement in his squeaky voice adorable.

"What's your name, little guy?"

"My human calls me Mr. Squeakers, but I prefer

the name Pip." Pip used his back leg to scratch behind his head. "What's your name?"

"Juniper." I gestured at the cage. "Does he keep you contained all the time?"

"He doesn't understand why I can't use a litter box like Mrs. Miller's cat." He sniffed the air. "At least that's what he says every time he lets me out for several minutes."

I unhooked the special lock on his cage and opened the door. I could relate to the feeling of being cooped up all the time. "You're welcome to come back with me to the swamp. I'm happy to grant you freedom."

Pip crawled out of the cage and jumped to the back of the couch. "I don't mind being a pet. How is it you can understand me? And what are you doing here?"

I waved my wand through the air. "The wand lets me communicate with nature and manipulate objects." I patted the pouch filled with fairy dust. "The dust allows us to give a sprinkle of good luck."

He crawled across the edge of the couch and back, standing on his hind legs. "You've come to the right house. I've never seen a human with so much bad luck."

I sat on the couch, pulling a pillow with seashells printed on it into my lap. "How so?"

"He's easily manipulated by his jerk of a boss and his not-so-nice ex-girlfriend. You should hear the way everyone who comes to the house talks to him. I can't imagine the other humans treat him any better once he leaves. Speaking of the house, he's on the verge of losing it. He's been on the phone with the bank and I heard him repeat the word 'foreclosure.' Someone stole money from his bank account and cleaned him out."

I rested my chin on my hand. "That's awful."

"It's weird that I know what all these things mean," he said.

I nodded. "It's the wand magic."

"I don't know what will happen to me if he loses his home. I've been raised by humans since birth. I've never had to jump from tree to tree and bury nuts." Pip jumped down to the coffee table and bumped into the vase of flowers.

It rattled on the tabletop and fell over, spilling flowers and water onto the floor.

"Uh oh," I said, dropping to my knees and picking up the roses. I stuck them back in the vase.

Pip jumped back to the couch. "Sorry."

The vase tumble had caused a screen to light up on the laptop on the coffee table. The screensaver had a picture of a white sailboat with a cursive *B* in the corner. I closed the top to put Pip and I back into darkness.

"John must like sailboats," I said and tapped the top of the laptop.

"The ex-girlfriend did. He doesn't really do anything but watch some show called TMZ," Pip said. "Do you have all these things in your fairy world?"

"Our world is similar to the human's, minus all the excessive electronics." I pointed to the laptop and oversized television hanging on the wall. "Our magic allows us to know what things are and how to use them, even if we've never actually touched them before."

Pip shook his head. "Magic is amazing."

"It comes with costs, and that's why we only use a pinch here and there."

He jumped to the coffee table and the vase shook again.

"We'd better get you back in your cage, and I'd better get my FE finished." I held out my hand for Pip but instead of jumping into my arms, he pointed behind me.

My stomach churned as fear curdled the berry soufflé I'd had for dinner. I turned slowly and found a man standing behind me in striped pajamas, his mouth hanging ajar.

I jumped back and reflexively my wings

unfurled, spreading behind me and lifting my feet off the ground.

The man, who I assumed to be John Bleaker, stumbled backwards and tripped over his own feet. He hit his head against the wall and a resounding thud followed. His eyes fluttered closed.

"You killed him!" Pip shouted.

"I didn't mean to!" I shouted back. I rushed to John's side and placed my hand on his chest. "He's still breathing."

"What are you going to do?" Pip jumped back and forth between the coffee table and the couch, once again knocking over the flowers.

My father would never forgive me for allowing a human to see our kind. Even if it had been by accident. Yet, he'd be the only one able to fix what I'd done. I grabbed a shaking Pip and nestled him in my arms, then I pulled out my wand. I tapped my head. "Home."

In an instant, I appeared back in the swamp. The portal sat open with a gaggle of palace guards surrounding my mother and father.

"It'll take all our wands to hold the portal open." Dad practically foamed at the mouth. "When I find that girl…"

My mom placed a hand on his arm. "I'm sure she's fine, dearest."

"I'm okay," I called out, my voice sounding as squeaky as Pip's.

Mom rushed forward and placed a hand on my cheek. "Please don't ever scare us like that again."

A rush of excited voices filled the air and my father waved a hand to silence them. He focused his glare on me. "Get to the palace right now."

"We can't," I said. "A human has seen my wings."

Chapter Four

The swamp echoed with the chattering of the guards. I'd seen my father angry on many occasions, but his speechlessness gave me a sense of dread I'd never felt before in his presence.

Mom pulled me into a quick hug. The scent of sweet jasmine surrounded us and her thick brown hair tickled my nose. She pushed me to an arm's length away and checked me with a quick bounce of her gaze up and down my body. "At least you're safe and unharmed. We'll fix this. Right, dear?" She glanced at my father who'd yet to do more than clench his fists at his side.

When my mother had spoken, the guards had once again gone silent. Mom and Dad moved to the side and their hushed discussion went on for several long minutes. I could tell my mom wasn't winning whatever argument they were having.

"Show me," my father said, the words coming out low and with sharp enunciation. My mother backed away from me and bowed her head. As much as she loved me, she wouldn't stand in the way of my father's rage against my actions.

Pip wiggled in my arms. "You're squishing me."

I relaxed my grip and my squirrely friend climbed to my shoulder, his claws pinching my skin.

Dad flicked his wrist and his wand appeared in his hand. "Amaranth, you will join us."

"Yes, sir," Amaranth came to stand beside me but didn't even flicker his eyes in my direction. I'd made a lot of mistakes tonight. I owed him an apology. That would come later.

Dad turned to my mother. "Take the remainder of the guards and close the portal. I will send a signal when we return."

"No," she said, her voice firm, yet she kept her eyes downcast. "I'll accompany you three. When we return, the four of us will have the power to open the portal and pass through. Then the rest of our kingdom can stay focused on their tasks."

Dad nodded and turned to the guards. "You have your orders." With another flick of his wrist, he moved his wand in a semi-circle and said, "Back."

As suddenly as I'd appeared in the forest, we

were back in the neighborhood of John Bleaker. We'd appeared in a cluster of trees in the conservation area to the left of the neighborhood.

I gasped at the activity outside of John Bleaker's house. Pip let out a chirp and clung to the side of my face.

Red and blue lights filled the night in blasts of blinding color. The lights belonged to several cars with the name Lilac Cove PD on the side. An ambulance and a firetruck were parked haphazardly beside them. Someone had draped yellow ribbon across the bushes in front of the door. I squinted and made out the words *crime scene*.

The entire neighborhood had come out for the light show, many of them dressed in robes and slippers.

"What have you done?" Dad asked.

Amaranth moved around us, his wings beating in an awkward rhythm. "Your majesty, we need to get you and the queen out of here."

Dad ignored him and bounced his wand against each of our heads. "Fit in."

My wings disappeared and my clothes changed to match the people standing nearby. The same happened for my mom, my dad, and Amaranth.

"Come with me and keep your mouths shut," Dad ordered.

We moved out of the brush and made our way to the group of people huddled together. Dad rubbed his eyes and yawned. He stopped by an elderly woman who cleaned her glasses with the edge of her robe. "What's going on?"

"Someone's murdered poor John Bleaker," she said and perched her glasses on the end of her nose. "I heard it over my personal police scanner a few minutes ago."

"That's not right," I blurted. "He was breathing when we left. Wasn't he, Pip?"

Pip blinked and squeaked. Then squeaked louder. He put his furry paw up to his neck and shook his little head. I couldn't understand him anymore but it appeared he could still understand me. When Dad hit us with his magic, he'd removed my ability to communicate with the one animal that could corroborate my story.

My dad's glare silenced any further defense.

The elderly woman wasn't fazed by my outburst and continued to supply us with information. "The dispatcher got a call from inside the house about an intruder dressed like a fairy and when they showed up—deader than a doornail."

"Exactly how dead is that?" I asked. Perhaps with the different levels of dead in the human world it could be reversed with wand magic or a bucket of fairy dust.

"Sweets," my mother interjected softly. "Dead is dead forever in any realm."

My heart sank. We couldn't fix this.

Amaranth once again moved between us and the humans. "The human police are asking questions of those standing outside. We need to leave before they make it over to us."

I stretched on my toes to see over his shoulder. Two men in uniforms with pens and notepads in hand moved through the crowd, stopping to ask questions.

We backed out of sight toward the deep shadows cast by the trees. Dad flicked our heads again and we each returned to our fairy forms and dress. Unfortunately, the wig had returned.

"I should speak to them," I said. "Tell them what I know."

"Absolutely not," Dad said.

"He was alive when I left or else he wouldn't have been able to make the call to their dispatch like the woman said." I pointed toward the woman who now spoke to a police officer.

"Even so," Amaranth interrupted, "you can't tell them who you are or why you were in the house. It's best we return to the swamp and leave this mess for the humans to clean up."

He placed a hand on my upper arm as if to direct me, and I pulled away. "No."

My father lifted his wand but before he could include me in his circular motion meant to send us back home, I put my hand over the end of it. "No," I said again. "We have to sort this."

"Juniper, the damage is done." My mother used her soft voice to soothe. "There is nothing we can do."

"Someone killed John Bleaker in the moments after I left. We can help find that person for the human police." I glanced back and forth between Amaranth and my mother. "It's the least we can do."

"There is no we, Juniper!" Dad bellowed my name as if all the anger he'd been holding back finally erupted to the surface. "You disobeyed your mother and I, your king and queen. You traveled into the human world and allowed one of them to see your wings. You will be held accountable for these actions."

Pip crawled behind my neck into my hair, and I understood his need to hide. My father was fierce on a good day, and this was not a good day.

"Daddy…" I started, unsure how to form an argument.

"Do not 'Daddy' me. You are not some insolent teenager in rebellion. You are a fully functioning adult godparent who made the choice to put yourself and our world in danger. That is not fitting of a princess of the fairy realm."

"Yes, Father. You're right. I was wrong." I appealed to his sense of reason. "And I am willing to face the consequences however you see fit back home. But right now, I need help setting things right for the human I failed."

"We're leaving," he said, the last of the angry tirade over with a whoosh of a sigh.

"No," I said again.

Amaranth stood behind my father. "Stop this at once. I cannot allow you to disobey the king."

"If you can't listen to me as my king, then listen to me as my father. You are the one who taught me right from wrong, and leaving is wrong," I pleaded. "How can you expect me to lead our kind one day if you don't listen to me now?"

He lowered his wand. "I have a kingdom to think of, as do you. We do not have the time to flit around and interfere with a murder investigation."

"You don't have to. I can do this by myself."

His jaw tensed. "Well then, future queen. How would you fix this?"

"With my wand and some dust." I patted my pouch. "I'll sprinkle and tap until the killer confesses and then hand him over to the proper authority."

He scoffed. "Your education into the human world is sorely lacking."

"That is your fault," I snapped.

My mother gasped.

"A mistake that I can easily rectify," he said. He waved his wand and my dust pouch disappeared. I reached in my pocket for Iris's wand but found it missing. With another flick of his wrist, my wings vanished and I dropped to the ground, my bare feet landing in a patch of wild ivy.

"What's this?" My mother asked, the horror in her eyes making them shine in the moonlight.

"She wants an education in the human world, then I'll give her one. It's only right that the future queen understand the people she's sworn to help." His thick eyebrows creeped up his forehead. "But she'll do it as one of them."

"She won't last an hour!" Mom cried. "She'll be defenseless."

Jeez, thanks for the vote of confidence, Mom.

Dad tossed me the tiniest of bags. "You'll have one dose of enchantment dust. You can use it however necessary or to return to the portal before the time allotted. I imagine you'll use it before the hour is up, but if you don't, know that you'll only have five days to clean up your mess before Amaranth will be sent to retrieve you. As the sole heir to the fairy godparent kingdom, your duty will be to return in five days' time and take your place in the throne room without hesitation. No more pining away at the fountain or having Iris sneak you books."

Seems Dad knew more about my interest in the human world than I gave him credit for. I crossed my arms. "I accept."

"Done," Dad said with his shoulders squared and jaw set firm.

Amaranth huffed out a held breath, but as a good soldier, he didn't argue with his king. I appeared to be the only one crazy enough to do that.

Dad expected me to change my mind or wilt or beg him not to leave. I'd show them all I was meant for more than sitting pretty on a throne.

"See you in five days." I turned my back to them and held my breath until my chest burned. The pent up breath came out in a whoosh. *I can do this.*

Chapter Five

My feet crunched the leaves and other foliage scattered across the ground. *Ouch.* Was that a stinging nettle? Prickles much like sharp stings blasted the length of the bottom of my right foot. *Dratted weeds.* I straightened my spine and kept my chin high. I wouldn't let Mom or Dad see me hopping on one foot and grunting in pain.

"Juniper." My mother called to me, but I didn't turn around. She poofed in front of me and pulled me into a quick hug. "Take this," she said, and slipped a small piece of rectangular paper into my hand. Her eyes silently pleaded with me as if to say stay safe before she tapped her head with her wand and simply said, "Home."

I turned to find my father and Amaranth no longer behind me. At least now I could scratch at my foot without total embarrassment. After a few scratches that didn't ease the stinging, I lifted the card into the moonlight to read the embossed writing. It had the name and address of a flower shop—*Fairyland Flowers, the loveliest flowers in Lilac Cove.* How could a flower shop help?

The asphalt of the road saw a welcome relief to my bare feet. I needed shoes, and soon. I glanced down at the sparkly dress I'd borrowed from Iris. Dad could have at least put me back in the human bedtime clothes. The lights from the police cars reflected off of the silver sequins. Pip had left my shoulder and now hung on to the fabric near my rear end. Fitting in would be difficult.

The cluster of people had thinned to less than ten onlookers, and an ambulance started a slow descent down the street. I knew enough to know that it contained John Bleaker's body. Why would anyone want to hurt a man who didn't have much of social life, according to his pet?

In my world, the fairies often squabbled over their land boundaries and who received the most prestigious fairy errands, but never in all my years had one killed another. Humans seem to do it all the time over the simplest of quarrels.

"I wish you still had the ability to speak," I turned my head and addressed Pip.

"Ma'am, are you okay?" A gruff man with a jagged scar across his cheek approached me. He glanced from my bare feet to the squirrel to my barely-hanging-on wig. "Do you need a hospital?"

"No, I'm fine." I took a deep steadying breath. "What I need is to speak to one of those police officers about John Bleaker's death."

"You know what happened?" he asked and moved closer to me. His unkempt hair fell over his forehead with a jerk of his head.

I took a tentative half-step backward. "Not exactly, but I think I have some information that could be very useful."

He cupped my arm above my elbow. "Listen, those police officers are very busy with other witnesses and securing the scene. Why don't you come with me?"

His question came out on a low grumble and my instincts told me he meant it in a way that I wouldn't be able to refuse. I jerked my arm twice to pull away, but his fingers tightened into my flesh.

"Let go," I said. Five minutes on my own and I was already being man-handled by a creep.

He yanked me close to his side. "My car's right over here. I'll take you where you need to go."

Panic shot through my body, mirroring the sting the nettles had caused. This man wasn't listening to me. "Please, let go."

The whimper in my voice must have alerted Pip and he leapt from my back thigh onto the scarred man's arm, biting him on his hand.

"What the heck!" The man swung his arm hard and flipped Pip into the air toward a police officer getting into the driver's side of his vehicle. The squirrel landed on all fours but didn't move.

I rushed to Pip and scooped him up in my arms. "My little hero. Are you hurt?"

"What's going on?" the police officer asked. A name tag on his shirt identified him as Officer Foster.

"That man," I pointed behind me.

"What man?" The officer asked, reaching out a hand to pull me to my feet.

I swiveled my head in every direction, but the creep had already hidden himself among the shadows. "He's gone."

Pip clung to the front of my dress while Officer Foster gave me the same once over as the guy with the scar. He started at my bare feet, then the squirrel, and finally his gaze landed and stayed on the wig. "Do you live around here, ma'am?"

I pulled at the wig until the pins freed it from my head. My real hair fell in a heap around my shoulders. "No."

His mouth pinched into a frown. "Can I escort you home?"

"I need to speak to someone in charge."

"In charge of what, exactly?" he asked.

"The murder. I can help you solve it."

Officer Foster cocked his head to the side much the same as Pip had done before we'd been able to communicate for the first time. "Did you witness what happened here tonight?"

If I had only stayed instead of poofing back home in a panic. My shoulders dropped with the heaviness of letting John down. "No."

"Did you by chance commit the crime that occurred here tonight?"

"I most certainly did not." I couldn't keep the indignation out of my voice.

"Then what information do you have?"

"I have Pip," I nodded at my chest, "and I've been inside the house before." I gestured toward John's house. "I know things." I tapped the side of my head like Iris had done earlier.

"What's that in your hand?" Officer Foster pointed to the card my mother had given me.

I turned it around to face him. "It's for a place called Fairyland Flowers."

Officer Foster's eyebrows rose and he nodded as if what I'd said finally put the pieces of a puzzle together. He waved his hand in a motion that captured me from head to toe. "Now, all of this makes sense. I thought her little get-together wasn't until next month. She always draws in all the weirdos."

"Excuse me?"

He opened the rear passenger door of the patrol car. "Get in. I'll give you a ride down to the station and we'll call Mrs. M for you."

I didn't know a Mrs. M or what he meant by *little get-together* but I did need a ride to their headquarters. Someone in charge would take me more seriously, if I could figure out how to share my information without giving away the fact that I was a fairy godparent.

Once inside the car, Pip nestled into my lap and closed his eyes. I could only imagine his exhaustion. He'd lost his owner and had protected a fairy all in one day. When my five days were up, I'd make sure he had a safe and happy home to return to. It'd be the least I could do for him.

The ride to the police station didn't take long and only after we arrived did I realize I'd had my first ever ride in a car. Not as fun as I'd thought car rides would be.

Officer Foster parked in front of a one-story red brick building. For it to be the middle of the night, the place was a bustle of activity. An older man and a younger woman walked in while Officer Foster let me out of the back seat. I followed him through the glass double doors and into a main waiting area. Three plastic chairs lined the wall.

He pointed to the one by a bulletin board with various posters tacked to it. One had a bright yellow headline that said *Five Most Wanted*. Pictures of five men who appeared to have done some nefarious deeds were lined up side-by-side.

I sat in the chair and waited. A man with close-clipped blonde hair spoke to the woman from the other side of the counter. He held an air of authority that made me think he was in charge. "Tell the mayor she should get her updates directly from Chief Rayburn, Brianna."

The blonde woman flicked her hair over her shoulder and leaned her elbows on the counter. I'd seen Iris do this when she wanted something from a male fairy. A flirting technique, she'd called it.

The woman he'd called Brianna pursed her lips and tapped long fingernails on the counter. "Mayor Caldwell and I have been working in the late hours of the evening and into early morning on the details for the May Day Festival. She's so upset, she had to go home and take a sleep aid."

Officer Foster sidled up next to the woman.

"Tell the mayor I'm happy to keep her apprised of the situation."

"Thank you so much, Officer Quick." The woman poked him with a finger and waltzed out of the police station.

"They can wait for the chief," the man behind the counter said again. His gaze flickered in my direction. "Who is that?"

Officer Foster straightened. "Found her at the crime scene trying to get attention. Someone needs to call Mrs. M to pick her up."

"Did you transport her without calling it in?" the other man asked.

"Relax, Callan. This isn't Atlanta." Foster cut his eyes at me before rolling them at the other man. "She's crazy, but all she's armed with is that squirrel."

The man squinted at me, taking in my appearance and the squirrel still asleep in my lap. "Wild animals aren't allowed in here."

I lifted my chin a notch. "Pip is a witness. Not a wild animal."

Officer Foster burst into a round of laughter. "See what I mean? Crazy." He disappeared behind the counter and sauntered to the back and out of sight.

So the man, Callan, not wearing a uniform or nametag wasn't in charge. He shook his head and lifted a finger for the older man waiting patiently to the side. When Callan disappeared from sight, the man sat down in a chair next to me.

He wore a three-piece suit and gray hair peeked out from his fedora-style hat. Perspiration settled around his forehead. Because of the fountain's ability to show us the human world, I knew that his style was both formal and outdated. He pointed to my lap. "That's a nice-looking squirrel you have there. Did you say his name was Pip?"

"Yes." I stroked Pip's back. "His owner called him Mr. Squeakers, but he prefers Pip."

The man removed his hat and placed it in his lap. "I had a pet skunk when I was a kid. Best little critter a farm boy could ask for." The man's voice was soft and his accent a light southern drawl.

"That's a nice story," I said. Pip rolled over onto his back and used his hind leg to scratch under his chin. We chuckled at the cuteness. "What are you doing at the police station so late?"

"I'm in Lilac Cove for a bit of pier fishing. The police chief has the keys to my Airbnb."

Before I could ask what an Airbnb was Callan came from behind the counter. "Sorry the chief couldn't be here to welcome you himself, but we seem to have a lot going on in our little town tonight. Here are the keys. Enjoy the cabin."

The older man placed his hat on his head and took the keys. He stood and smiled down at me. "Nice to meet you, Miss…?"

"Juniper. And you are?"

"You can call me Vinnie."

With that, he exited, and I was left as the sole focus of Callan. He wore a wrinkled button up shirt over a pair of dark jeans. His eyes were a soft blue color set against a deep tan, but the distrust in them made his gaze harsh, which matched his stern frown. "Do you have a last name, Juniper?"

"No."

He pressed his lips together and studied my face. "You don't have a last name, or you're not going to tell me?"

The doors swung open and a teenaged girl rushed into the lobby. "Ms. Emory woke me and gave me the news. Lilac Cove's very first murder! Did you get to see the body, Uncle Callan?"

Callan paled at the sight of her. He glanced at his watch and back at her. "It is two a.m., Olivia. You should be in bed. How did you get here?"

She shrugged off a backpack and set it on the floor. "I rode my bike."

He pointed to the chair beside me, his finger shaking. "Sit. Now."

Olivia slumped into the chair and poked her lips

into a full pout. "I never get to be a part of anything cool."

"Story of my life," I said before I could stop the words from escaping.

She glanced at me and her gaze settled on Pip. Her expression changed from sullen to excitement within a millisecond. "Is that a real squirrel?"

"It is. His name is Pip."

She reached over and gave him a scratch on his furry belly. "Is he the reason you've been arrested?"

"I haven't been arrested." At least I didn't think that's what had happened. "I'm trying to help solve a crime, but Officer Foster won't listen to me."

Olivia nodded, giving me a once over. "It's hard to take you seriously dressed you are. Plus, you aren't wearing any shoes."

Shoes. No wonder everyone stared at my feet. How had I missed that that one clothing item gave a person leverage in the human world?

"How do I get shoes?" I asked. "A pair that will make everyone take me seriously."

She stood and shouted over the counter. "Hey, Uncle Callan? Can I show this lady to the lost and found? She needs shoes."

He leaned over the counter, and from his pensive expression, I could see him assessing if I was a danger to his niece. I didn't blame him. In fact, it made him all the more attractive as a human male.

"It's fine," he said gesturing to a hallway. "But don't close the door behind you."

I cradled Pip and followed Olivia down the hallway. We came to a door labeled *Janitorial.* "My name's Juniper, by the way."

Olivia opened the door and flipped the light switch. "Nice to meet you, Juniper. Olivia."

"Lovely name. How old are you?" We walked into a small square room with a deep sink on the wall near the far corner. Mops and well-worn brooms had been propped against another corner.

The girl pushed her glasses up her nose and smiled. "Turned fourteen last month." She pushed aside more cleaning supplies and pulled forward a large plastic container. She gasped and threw her body over the top of the container, grabbing something on the other side. "I thought I'd lost you."

"What did you find?" I asked.

"My collection of Sherlock Holmes. He's only the greatest detective ever." She hugged the book to her chest. Then she pushed the lid off of the container and revealed a various assortment of clothing.

"I haven't read that one." I dug through the shirts and pants, coming up with a flannel shirt, workman coveralls, and a pair of boots. "How did someone lose all these clothes?"

"My uncle says it's best not to ask those questions." She settled on another box nearby. "He used to be a detective in Atlanta. Now he works dispatch. That's why I have to stay the nights with Ms. Emory. But I don't need a babysitter."

Pip awoke from his nap and I set him down on a cardboard box with "Christmas Decorations" written on the side. He stared at Olivia with either curiousness or a tinge of fear. I couldn't be certain which, but he didn't run and hide.

I shrugged into the long-sleeved shirt and pulled the coveralls over my dress. They would have to do for now. Iris was more the fashion maven when it came to keeping up with the human and fairy world of clothes and trends. I usually wore whatever was set out for me by my mother.

The boots were large and my feet slid around in them. "I don't think these are the right size."

Olivia took in my appearance and wrestled to keep a smile off of her face. "You do look less ridiculous than before."

That was something.

I trudged behind her back to the front area and once again the man she'd called Uncle Callan was occupied with a visitor. This one was a woman who had kinky gray curls that hung down her back almost to her waist. She wore a bright purple top with bold green pants. Her shoes were white canvas with pictures of butterflies.

Callan pointed to me. "That's her."

The woman turned and when our eyes met, my breath caught in my throat. My pulse picked up to an abnormally quick pace. I stumbled toward her but any reservations I had about her identity lifted as she smiled. I'd only ever seen a portrait, but I'd studied it long and hard, always wondering about her.

I found my voice as I reached out to her. "Aunt Mossandra?"

Chapter Six

Olivia danced around us in a circle. "Mrs. M is your aunt? How lucky are you! She's the coolest. Everyone loves her."

Callan came around the counter and pulled his precocious niece to the side. "Come on. Let's see if Officer Foster can give you a ride back to Emory's house. I'm sure she's worried sick, if she's even noticed you've escaped again."

Aunt Mossandra's smile dropped as the tiniest bit of sadness worked its way into her eyes. She reached out and pulled both of my hands into hers. "If you're here like *this*, then that means your father is throwing his weight around again."

I glanced at Olivia and Callan, who tried to look as if they weren't listening to every word we spoke. It didn't matter how well my aunt fit in or if she'd even told humans about her true nature, I wouldn't betray my kind. "Let's just say Dad is a little upset with me. It'll pass."

Aunt Mossandra looked past me at our eavesdroppers. "I'll take Olivia back to Emory's house, Callan. She can regale us with tales of the latest mystery she's reading."

Olivia wedged between us and we dropped hands. "Haven't you heard? John Bleaker's been murdered in his home. We have our very own real-life mystery in town." She nodded toward me. "Juniper has information about it, but Officer Quick wouldn't take her seriously."

"That's Officer Foster to you!" The officer's shout carried from somewhere in the back of the police station. "And we deal in facts in this police station. Not psychic feelings."

Callan and Mossandra took in my new outfit with varying degrees of concern. Pip clung to the front of me and swished his bushy tail with two swift jerks.

Aunt Mossandra's brows knitted together. "That's awful about John. Who would do such a thing?"

"What does Officer Foster mean, 'psychic feelings'?" Callan asked.

Aunt Mossandra tilted her head back and let out

a rancorous and absolutely fake laugh. "You really are too much, dear. Did you tell the police you were psychic?"

"Not exactly."

"Hey *dispatch*, the phone is ringing." Officer Foster's voice boomed from the back again. "Leave the actual police work to the police."

Callan tossed a glare in the other man's direction. "I've got to get back to work. Thanks for giving Olivia a ride, Mrs. M. I'll take her bike with me after my shift." He turned to me and lowered his voice. "If you truly have information that would help the case, you should come back tomorrow when the police chief is here. Chief Rayburn is with the sheriff and county detective now, but he'll take whatever you have to say under consideration."

I nodded and noted that he acted less dismissive of me than before.

"Come along, my dear." Aunt Mossandra cupped my elbow and steered me toward the door. "I'm sure once you've had some rest, you'll rethink getting involved in this mess."

Olivia yawned, her mouth bobbing up and down on our way out the door.

The three of us stopped in front of a parked monstrosity. Aunt Mossandra's brownish-tan colored car could be considered a boat in terms of modern vehicles. On the hood, the paint had faded away in some areas and there were rust-rimmed holes on the driver's side door. I'd never seen anything quite so ugly. And I'd seen trolls.

She caught my hesitance. "Don't you just love it, my dear? It's a 1972 Ford Galaxie." She reached through the window and opened the rear passenger door with the inside handle. "I have some things for my flower shop in the front seat, so you'll have to sit in the back with Olivia."

My second car ride. I'd seen cars of all shapes and sizes through the courtyard fountain, and during fairy training we'd been taught to avoid them like the plague. More than one poor fairy godparent in our long history had met their demise thanks to the front grill of a car.

I slid across the seat, careful not to add more damage to the already ripped vinyl interior. The front seat held hand-painted flowerpots stacked neatly together and seatbelted in with the lap belt. Pip jumped off my coveralls and situated on the shelf-like area beneath the rear window.

Olivia scooted in beside me, the excitement and lack of sleep wearing her down. She pushed her glasses up and rubbed her eyes. "Our very first murder mystery in Lilac Cove." She lifted the book in her hands. "Exactly like in my books."

"Not exactly, sweets." My aunt dropped into the driver's seat and tilted the rearview mirror to give us both a stern look. "Someone in our community has lost his life, and we should always treat that with respect."

Aunt Mossandra brought the car to life and the engine roared like a beast.

"We should help the police," Olivia countered, lowering her voice so only I could hear.

"How do we do that?" All I wanted was to help find justice for John.

She passed me the collection of Sherlock Holmes stories. "Study this and meet me at my house tomorrow afternoon. I have school, but I'll be done by four." She flipped open the front cover. "Here's my address."

"I appreciate the book." I didn't want to break it to her that getting a child involved in a murder investigation was not an option I'd consider.

We drove down the street where John Bleaker had lived a full boring life only hours before. Aunt Mossandra parked in front of a house across the street. The woman from earlier who'd told Dad about John's death walked out onto her front porch and waved.

Instead of waiting for the door to be opened, Olivia crawled out the window. "Thanks for the ride."

"Make sure to apologize to Emory for sneaking out," my aunt reminded her.

I couldn't pull my gaze away from John's now darkened house. The police tape remained, but the circus of vehicles and lights had cleared out. Pip low crawled toward my head and nuzzled my cheek.

"I live behind my flower shop on the square in the middle of town. You're going to love it."

I flipped through the pages of Olivia's book as we drove toward the heart of Lilac Cove. Officer Foster had called me a psychic, but that couldn't be farther from the truth. Yet, I couldn't tell anyone the actual truth, and in order to share my information, I needed a cover story. Posing as a psychic might work.

But first, one baffling mystery at a time. I wanted some answers from my aunt.

She must have sensed my gaze focused on the back of her head. "What's going through your mind, my dear?" Aunt Mossandra guided her boat of a car into a parking spot in front of Fairyland Flowers. It groaned when she put it in park and cut the engine. She twisted to face me and rested her hands over the edges of the front bench seats.

"Have you been here in Lilac Cove the entire time? This close to the kingdom? Why didn't you come home or to visit?" My questions came out in a rush of garbled words.

"Let's have a cup of tea inside, and I'll do my best to explain."

Pip grabbed on to my shoulder and I pulled the book tight against my chest. My feet still slid around in the ridiculously big boots, so I kicked them off before following her through the door. The strong scent of perfumed roses tickled my nose. An overhead florescent light fixture in the far corner gave off enough light so that I could see the outlines of potted palms and ferns.

Aunt Mossandra led me through a path of containers. Upon closer inspection, I could see that they'd been made into fairy gardens. Through a sturdy door that separated the flower shop from the next room, I realized we'd come into an open one-room apartment. Painted pictures of fairies and a few of Aunt Mossandra dressed like a fairy adorned the walls.

"Do you even try to hide the fact that you're a fairy?" I stood in front of a picture of my aunt and several other women, all wearing bright pink fairy wings.

"The best way to fit in is to stand out," she said on a light chuckle. "The weirder I act, the more the humans accept me as one of them." She bustled around her kitchenette, adding water to two teacups and putting them in the microwave.

"Why are you here?" I sat at a half table with two matching folding chairs.

She held up a finger, silently asking me to wait a minute. After the microwave let out a ding, she removed both cups and added a tea bag. "I hope chamomile is okay. At first, I thought it would help calm your nerves but after seeing you, I'm amazed at how well you're integrating into the human world." She placed a saucer and cup in front of me. "It took me weeks to get inside a car. And already you've been inside two."

Before she sat down, Aunt Mossandra pulled a ream of crackers from a cabinet. She opened them and sat them on the table. "There you are, Mr. Squeakers."

"He prefers Pip, Aunt Mossandra," I corrected her.

Pip jumped off my shoulder and pulled a cracker from the sleeve. He broke off chunks and crammed them into his mouth.

"I'd love it if you called me Mossy. Many of the folks in town prefer Mrs. M, but that's too formal, and you'll get very tired of saying Aunt Mossandra every time you want my attention."

"Okay, Mossy." I took a sip from the tea. "Let's

start from the beginning. How did you end up in Lilac Cove and owning a flower shop?"

"I met a man." She smiled down at her tea. "It almost always starts with a man."

Chapter Seven

"You're no longer a true fairy godparent because you wanted to date the chief of police?"

"Well, it didn't start with Greg. He's my chosen significant other for this year."

Hello. And what? "You choose a different man each year?"

"I like to try them out." She lifted her foot and rotated her ankle. "Like different pairs of shoes."

I buried my face in my hands. "You're saying my grandparents banished you because…"

She poked at my hands so I'd look at her. "I like human men, my dear. And I refused to marry the fairy I'd been betrothed to since birth. In fact, I refuse to get married at all. What's the point?"

I sipped my tea. "Huh."

She sat back, her eyes a shade darker than mine yet full of life and mischief. Nothing in her tone or body language suggested she regretted the choice she'd made.

"What does my dear brother tell everyone?" she asked.

The teacup rattled the saucer when I put it down. "That you wanted to be a part of the human world and he couldn't have you going back and forth."

She waved a hand in the air. "That's not too far from the truth. I was forced to choose. I don't think fairies should have to."

"Don't you miss home?"

"I've made a home here. I have a successful business and friends that are as close as family. I'm happy." She leaned forward. "We've talked enough about me. Why are you here? Does it have something to do with John and an errand?"

"Dad doesn't let me godparent like everyone else. So I borrowed Iris's fairy errand—she's my best friend—and I got distracted with all the wonderful things I've only seen through the fountain." Pip finished his crackers and settled near my hands. "Because I didn't give John Bleaker his sprinkle of fairy dust, he didn't get the luck he needed for his interview this morning. And someone killed him."

Mossy stared across the room and tapped her fingers against her lips. Finally, she shrugged. "I don't know how John being murdered adds up to you not providing luck for an interview."

"I don't know yet, but deep in my gut, I know it's my fault. I wanted to give the police all the information I have, but Dad said we had to leave things as they are. What if his killer is never brought to justice because of all my interference?"

"You made it inside his house?"

"Yes. He woke up and saw me with my wings."

"Juniper."

"I know. The first rule of fairy godparents is if you get caught, *hide your wings and wait for the king.*" We'd sung the words as a nursery rhyme many times as children.

"What did you see that you think will help the police?"

"I don't know. Yet. But there has to be something that I saw that can be useful." I played with the teacup handle. "Dad has given me five days to fix this mistake."

"I bet his highness said you wouldn't make it an hour."

Our chuckles mingled. "Something close to that."

"There's no way to share your information

without having to have a plausible explanation for why you know the things you know."

"I thought about that. The other officer mentioned something about me being a psychic. I can use that as a cover to explain what I know."

"A psychic?"

"Maybe I can pretend to be one that talks to animals? Pip told me a lot about John before Dad removed our ability to communicate."

Mossy eyed the snoozing squirrel. "Did he now?"

A round of knocks came from the back door near the kitchenette. Mossy glanced at her watch. "I wonder who that could be? It's not even five a.m. yet."

She opened the door to find an older gentleman who wore the same police uniform as Officer Foster. I placed the age difference between the two men to be about thirty years, but I'd swear they were related.

"Mossy," he said and glanced past resting his gaze on me. "Hello, miss. Quick told me that you'd come to visit your aunt."

The man moved into the apartment, and the third person made the apartment less homey and more cramped. Mossy gestured to him. "Juniper, this is Chief Greg Rayburn."

He held out his hand, and I stood to give it a

quick shake.

"Who is Quick again?" I asked.

"Sorry. I meant Officer Foster. He's my nephew. I've always called him by his nickname."

"Did you come to talk to Juniper?" Mossy asked.

"Actually, I'm here for you. The county detective would like to ask you some questions about John."

"What does Mossy know about John Bleaker?" I asked.

"That's between the detective and Mossy for now. I'm sorry for the inconvenience." He nodded toward the door, the discomfort showing in the redness on his face. "I told him I'd swing around and pick you up."

"Wait," I started when he turned his back to open the door again. Callan said the police chief is the one I should talk to. Now was as good a time as any. Before I could ask him, Mossy rushed to me and pulled me into an uncomfortable hug with my arms pinned at my side.

"Keep what you know to yourself for now," she whispered against my ear. She picked up her purse from a side table beside the bed. "Get some rest, my dear. I'll be back in no time and we can plan out the rest of your visit."

Unease filled me as they left me standing next to the table. Why did the county detective think Mossy had information about John Bleaker? Why wouldn't she want me to share what I know? Pip pulled me out of my thoughts as he scratched the back of his head with his hind paw. He immediately fell back asleep. Did squirrels always sleep this much? I smoothed the fur on the top of his head with one finger.

I glanced around the room, my first instinct to snoop. *The snooping is what started this mess.* Mossy had a bed big enough for one person and a flower-patterned love seat against the far wall. Unlike John's house, she didn't have a large television on the wall or a laptop on the coffee table. Since I couldn't imagine sleeping, I grabbed Olivia's book and curled my legs under me on the sofa.

After the first two stories, I found Olivia's assessment about Sherlock Holmes being the greatest detective to be true. He used his powers of intense observation to detect clues that others thought were insignificant. Well, I could do that. I flipped the page to the next story.

Two hours and one Sherlock Holmes immersion later, and my eyelids grew heavier than I'd ever remembered them feeling.

I swore I closed them for only a few seconds, but when I opened them again, the sunlight shone bright through the one window in the room. Why hadn't Chief Rayburn returned with Mossy? Or had he and she was in the flower shop? I tilted my head to listen for sounds coming from the front area. "Mossy?" I called out.

No response. Maybe she couldn't hear me from back here.

I stretched and found Pip had curled into my lap. At some point I'd placed the book on the floor in front of us. He jumped down, bumping the book and the front flap opened to Olivia's name and address scribbled in the front. I toyed with the edges of the blanket. I didn't know anyone else in Lilac Cove and she seemed to know more than a fourteen-year-old should. If I couldn't find Mossy, then maybe I could find my way to her house.

First, I had to change out of the coveralls. Behind a sliding screen I found a clawfoot bathtub, a toilet, a hanging rack full of clothes, and a rectangle bin filled to the brim with shoes. All sorts of shoes. I tried not to focus on how my aunt had compared men to switching pairs.

Mossy and I were similar in build and shoe size, so I helped myself to a blue dress with a matching sweater. In the bin, I found a pair of dark blue sneakers with a star on the side and *Converse* written on the tongue. They appeared to be decent walking shoes that would also inspire confidence, so I slipped into them.

Near the bed, she had hooks with several bags hanging from them. I put my one dose of fairy dust in the side pocket. Best to keep it close. I opened the main zipper and held the bag wide for Pip. "I can't have you riding on my clothes all day. The humans give us funny looks."

He chittered and jumped inside, turning around a few times before popping his head back out.

I made my way to the front flower shop and, as I'd feared, the lights were still off and the sign on the front door still turned to closed. A woman pressed her face against the front glass.

I unlatched the deadbolt and the woman stepped inside. "Hello."

She clasped her hands in front of her and gave me a stiff smile. "I heard our Mossy had a visitor. I'm Gladys."

"My name is Juniper. Mossy is my aunt." I reached out my hand the same as Chief Rayburn had done earlier when we'd exchanged greetings. "How did you know I was here?"

Gladys squeezed my hand and didn't let go. "Emory called me first thing this morning. Olivia couldn't stop singing your praises after you and Mossy dropped her off in the wee hours. I volunteered to come check you out in person."

Pip squeaked and chittered and Gladys finally let go of my hand. "Is that John Bleaker's pet squirrel? How did you get him?"

"I found him outside after my dad dropped me off." The lie rolled off my tongue with such ease that I surprised myself.

Gladys raised her pencil-drawn eyebrow. She glanced around the flower shop, picking a few buds from their stems. "Interesting."

"My aunt isn't here."

"Oh, I know dear. She's still at the sheriff's office with that detective. But don't worry, none of us believe that she killed poor John." She straightened her sweater. "Wouldn't you already know that, since you have psychic abilities?"

Gladys had a lot of useful information, but something about the way she eyed me with suspicion told me she didn't believe my lie about how I'd found Pip. Or that I might be a psychic. She didn't trust me.

"So do you have any real knowledge about what happened last night?" she asked.

Mossy had asked me to not say anything and for now I'd keep to that. "No."

Disappointment flooded her features.

"Do you know where this address is?" I asked, changing the subject by opening the book to the inside front cover.

"Of course. Will you be driving or walking?"

"Walking."

"You'll find there isn't much to Lilac Cove. There's the square, and then a half-mile that way," she pointed to the area behind me, "is the beach. The police station and city hall are a good hike to the right once you walk out the door. All the housing communities are to the left. The streets signs and house numbers are clear as day once you start walking a straight path down the sidewalk. There are only about seven hundred people who live here, so if you get lost anyone will be able to set you straight."

"Thank you for your help, Gladys." I followed her out the door and she waved at me with the back of her hand.

I headed in the direction she'd indicated, but I still hadn't a clue as to how I'd help solve John Bleaker's murder, or to convince the police that Mossy couldn't possibly be involved.

Chapter Eight

I crossed against the crosswalk light since I'd been standing on the corner for several minutes without seeing a single car and the light had refused to budge even though I pushed the little knob over and over.

A prickle started at the base of my spine and traveled toward my neck. I turned my head to find the man with the scar from the evening before leaned against a silver sedan. He was parked in front of a store that said *Liam's Hardware*.

I quickened my pace and, after a few steps, snuck another look in his direction. He didn't smile or wave or acknowledge me in any way other than to stare. I made a mental note to ask Mossy and the police chief about him when I saw them next. The scar would be distinct enough that if he were a resident of Lilac Cove, they'd know him. In the meantime, if he even moved like he would approach me, I'd put the *Converse* to good use and run.

Pip chittered in a series of clicks. The staring man made him nervous too. I gave him a reassuring pat on the head.

After two blocks of residential area, I found the street that belonged to Olivia. I double-checked the numbers on the house with the ones scribbled inside the book. She'd said I could meet her after four in the afternoon. From the position of the sun, the way I'd been taught to tell time in the fairy realm, I put the time at four fifteen.

I'd slept on Mossy's couch much longer than I'd first realized. What a waste of my first day.

Olivia and her uncle lived in a one-story stucco home painted a light blue with a two-car garage. The other homes on the street matched the style with different colors such as yellow and tan. The grass crunched with each step until I reached the walkway in front of the door.

I knocked four times before I pressed the doorbell.

Callan snatched open the door after the third doorbell ring with a, "What the heck do you want?"

He wore a wrinkled T-shirt and striped pajama bottoms. His blonde hair was mussed and fell over his forehead, giving him a boyish charm. The scowl on this face, however, did not.

"I'm sorry," I said. "Did I wake you?"

He crossed his arms and leaned against the doorjamb. "I work twelve-hour shifts as dispatch, so I sleep most of the day. What can I do for you?"

I lifted the book. "I came to return this to Olivia."

"She's grounded." He reached for the book, but I pulled it back against my chest.

"I, um, was hoping she could show me around town. She's been the friendliest person I've met so far."

My comment about friendly people hit him and his expression softened. "Emory caught her trying to sneak into John's this morning before school, so she won't be going anywhere for a while. She's not allowed out of her room."

Sherlock would start from the crime scene, too. Very smart of Olivia, but also dangerous for a child. I should go there next, if I could find my way back.

Callan waited for me to say something more. Probably goodbye. But he was the one who suggested I speak to the chief, so perhaps he had other useful advice I could rely upon. "The police chief took my aunt for questioning early this morning. She's not back yet. I have to help her if I can."

"I heard." He straightened and moved to the side, running a hand through his hair. "Why don't you come in for a cup of coffee, and I'll tell you what I know."

"Thank you." I followed him through a small foyer and through a modest living room to the kitchen.

"Have a seat." He gestured to a round kitchen table with four chairs. "How do you like your coffee?"

"I don't know. I've never had coffee." I could tell Pip had fallen asleep again, so I set my bag gently on the floor beside my feet.

"Where did you say you were from?"

"I didn't, really." I noticed a picture on the wall with a younger Olivia sitting in a woman's lap. "Is that Olivia's mom?"

"Yeah. She died a year ago, and Olivia came to live with me."

"Where is her father?"

"He's a deadbeat. We don't talk about him."

"I don't mean to pry. She's a very smart girl."

"Too smart."

I sipped the coffee and cringed. "Oh, that's bitter."

He chuckled and opened the refrigerator. "I

suggest condensed milk and sugar to start."

After he poured in milk from a can and added a spoonful of sugar, I tried it again. "Mm. Much better. Olivia told me you used to be a detective, but now you work dispatch for the police station."

He sat in the chair opposite me and took a long drag of his coffee. "I worked the criminal investigations division in Atlanta for a few years. A few years were all it took to wear me down."

"There's a lot of bad in the world," I agreed. "But my aunt's not one of those people. Why do they think she knows anything about John Bleaker's murder?"

"I'm going to tell you some things that I probably shouldn't, but since Officer Foster has already told half the town, you have a right to know too. Your aunt dated John last year and they parted on bad terms. At the crime scene, they found flowers delivered from your aunt to John and the vase had been smashed. Also, when John called the station he mentioned that he saw a fairy in his house before the call disconnected. Your aunt often dresses with fairy wings to promote her flower business."

If Mossy had already moved on to the next man in her life, why would she care about a relationship that ended badly last year? "None of those things suggests she'd break into his house in the middle of the night. Bad relationship or not."

"I agree. That's why I don't think you need to be worried. The county detective will send her home before too much longer."

"Can I pick your detective brain for a minute?"

"I see my niece has infected you with her inquisitiveness." He propped his elbows on the table. "But okay, go ahead."

"If you were the detective on this case, where would you start?" When his eyebrows dropped into a frown, I added, "Hypothetically speaking, of course."

"It always comes down to motive, means, and opportunity." He'd raised his hand and ticked off his fingers as he'd said each one. "Motive would be the reason someone would want him dead. This is the biggest piece of the puzzle. Even with a crime of passion or an incident of accidental manslaughter, there's still a motive for what pushed the person to react in such a violent manner."

I set the book down on the table. "How would you determine a motive?"

"I'd start with those closest to him and work my way out. The people most likely to have a motive would be a significant other, co-workers, bosses, neighbors. It's possible it's a stranger-related killing, but those usually go along with robberies gone wrong."

"How well did you know John?"

"Not well at all. I mostly keep to myself and fail at keeping Olivia out of trouble. There's not much time for socializing otherwise."

I smiled at him. "That's a shame."

He smiled back. "Anyway, I'm on shift tonight and need another few hours of sleep before dinner."

"Thank you for not dismissing my concerns."

"Our department worked with a psychic or two in Atlanta. I learned to keep an open mind about everything." He ran a hand through his hair and kept his expression neutral. "How long are you in town? Maybe we could have coffee again?"

"Five days, unfortunately, but if I can assist with bringing John's murderer to justice before then, I'd be happy to have another coffee."

"Murder investigations can take months. Without solid evidence—up to a year. Unless you have had a vision of the murderer and a confession, I'd suggest leaving the police work to the police."

I didn't blame him for not understanding, but I didn't have months. I only had five days to find the murderer, and I wouldn't give up until I did.

Chapter Nine

I thanked Callan again and he shut the door hard behind me. Where did I go next? I could check back at the flower shop to see if Mossy had returned.

A *pssst pssst* drew my attention to the corner of the house. Olivia stuck her head out of a window and motioned me forward.

"I heard you're grounded."

"Yeah. I guess sneaking out twice in one twenty-four hour period was pushing it." She tossed her hair out of her face and adjusted her glasses. "I heard you talking with Uncle Callan about motives."

"How do I find out the closest people to John?"

"The gossip club will have all the latest information. They're probably still at the little diner on the corner of the square, if you hurry."

"What's a gossip club?"

"Ms. Emory, Ms. Gladys, and Ms. Allondra get together for high tea in the Corner Café at five p.m. most weekdays and discuss everyone in town. What happened to Mr. Bleaker will be at the top of their list."

"I've met Emory and Gladys. I don't think Gladys trusts me."

"Tell them something that no one else knows and they'll be your best friend for life."

"Make them the top gossipers, you mean?"

"Exactly."

Olivia dipped back inside and tilted her head. "I think my uncle is coming. Once I'm off house arrest, I'll find you."

She shut the window and Pip and I followed our route back to the town's square. The man with the scar was no long sitting in front of the hardware store. I glanced around to make sure he hadn't moved to the other side of the street.

Fairyland Flowers still had the closed sign turned and the lights were off. Mossy's big beast of a car sat in the same parking spot as the night before. No Mossy. With my confidence slipping, I strode past and to the diner called Corner Café.

The gossip club would only share information if I shared it with them first. What did I have that could be of use? Mossy had asked me to keep the private information about John quiet, and I didn't want to go against her wishes while she defended herself to the police.

Did I know something else from the short amount of time I'd been in Lilac Cove?

The Corner Café had a black and white striped awning over the door. Swirly script announced the opening and closing times, as well as a strict no pet policy.

"I think you'd better keep hidden for now, Pip." I pushed his little head into the bag and zipped it three-fourths of the way closed. His displeasure became apparent with excited chitters, but he calmed after a minute.

The inside of the café's décor matched the awning in that it had black and white pictures, tablecloths, chairs, and even the server behind the tall glass counter wore a black apron over a white shirt.

The only patrons in the café were the three gossip mavens Olivia had asked me to seek out. They each wore brightly colored dresses in pink, purple, and orange. Each wore a hat that matched their outfits and the fresh flowers Gladys had picked from the shop.

Emory, in the pink, waved to me. "Join us for a cup of tea and a scone, why don't you? Our treat."

The invite hadn't taken long. I sat in the

unoccupied chair between Emory and the woman who wore the purple dress that I assumed to be Allondra.

"Hello."

Allondra pulled a vial of hand sanitizer from her purse and rubbed it on her dark skin. "We hear your aunt is still being questioned by the police."

"Juniper claims she doesn't know anything," Gladys interjected.

"I might know something," I said and smoothed my skirt. "I'm not sure I should say anything though."

"You're amongst friends." Emory pushed a teacup toward me and used a kettle from the middle of the table to fill it with hot water. After she set a tea infuser inside, she offered me cream. "We consider Mossy one of our closest friends."

I poured a few drops of cream into my cup and bounced the infuser up and down to release the full flavor of the tea leaves. "I know that Mossy dated John Bleaker last year."

"We know that already," Gladys said, her thin eyebrow lifted high as if to tell me to try again.

Undeterred, I did just that. "I know that she sent him flowers yesterday."

"And."

"They were yellow. The color of friendship."

That one small extra detail couldn't hurt Mossy, but the three women glanced at each other as if I'd told them something of importance.

"Yellow is the first step in reconciliation," Allondra said.

"What if John denied her and she bopped him on the head?" Gladys added.

"What? No!" What kind of friends would think that giving someone flowers meant they would kill them?

"What else do you know?" Emory put a scone on a bright white saucer and shoved it toward me.

My throat tightened. I broke off the edge of the scone and put it in my purse for Pip to stall for time. Anything I said could be construed as a reason that Mossy could be the killer. I had to find a way to put other suspects in their line of fire. "I know that he had a job interview this morning. That he had an ex-girlfriend that bossed him around. That it couldn't have been my aunt."

Would one of those things do it?

"John was leaving the mayor's office?" Allondra asked. "That's a surprise. He loved having access to all the goings-on in the entire town. It's like a mini-throne without the actual work of being in charge."

Gladys flicked a finger at the door. "Speaking of ex-girlfriends, here comes John's most recent."

I swiveled my head to see the flirty woman from last night with shiny blonde hair enter the café. Callan had called her Brianna. She wore a black dress and oversized dark sunglasses. Her lips were colored a dark red. She spoke to the server behind the counter. "I'm here for the mayor's dinner."

When Brianna saw us staring at her she wiggled her fingers with a wave and gave us a tight smile.

Emory tsked a couple of times. "She doesn't seem overly broken up about John's death."

"She sleeps around more than your aunt," Allondra said in a tone loud enough to carry to the glass counter.

The other women shushed her but I could tell from the server's expression that both she and Brianna had heard Allondra's declaration.

Brianna paid for the meal but didn't give us another glance as she marched through the door. Officer Foster arrived just in time to hold it for her and he gave her a nod before watching her walk down the sidewalk.

Gladys immediately called out to him. "Officer Foster, sweetheart. Don't you look exhausted from keeping the streets of Lilac Cove safe."

He sauntered over, hands on his utility belt. "Yes, ma'am. I've been running around all night trying to help the county detective. The mayor would prefer we handle this case ourselves, but the sheriff told her she didn't have final say."

Officer Foster did a quick double take when he noticed me sandwiched between Gladys and Allondra. "If it isn't our new town psychic. You've cleaned up a bit since last night. Are you reading these ladies' tea leaves?"

Allondra gasped. "Are you a psychic? My Auntie Eleanor had the power of sight." She shoved her hand in my face. "Read my palm."

I pulled her hand away from my nose. "I'm not that sort of psychic."

This time both of Gladys's eyebrows rose. The effort made a ripple of lines on her forehead. "Then what kind are you?"

I'd wanted to wait until I had the police chief's attention, but maybe having Officer Foster's attention could be just as good. He seemed motivated to search for the truth. Even if it was to please the mayor.

Pip made a squeak and I lifted my bag to the table. *Here goes nothing.* "I can talk to animals. This is John's pet squirrel, Pip. I think he called him Mr. Squeakers, but that's not what he likes to be called."

Officer Foster's jaw swung open and for several seconds he didn't make a sound. Finally, he pulled out his notepad from the top pocket of his shirt. "We found an empty cage, but we weren't certain what type of animal had been inside. How did you get him?"

"I found him outside last night, or rather, he found me," I lied.

Officer Foster yanked a chair from another table and set it down beside Allondra. He sat and clicked the top of a pen, poised to take notes. "Tell me everything you know."

I hesitated.

Emory nudged my arm. "Well, tell him, Juniper. This could help get your aunt out of trouble. Isn't that what you want?"

"Well…" I stalled and wracked my brain for how to use this situation to my advantage. "Pip says that we need to visit the crime scene before he'll give me more information."

Officer Foster grimaced. "I'm not so sure I can do that."

"Imagine if you solve the case for the mayor," Gladys said to him. "Then when the chief retires, she'll likely endorse you as his replacement."

I appreciated her encouragement and wondered at her change of heart about trusting me.

The police officer's eyes rounded with the possibility. "The crime scene technicians have removed the evidence and taken photographs of everything. I can't see the harm in letting you inside, as long as you don't touch anything."

I stamped down the twinge of guilt that threatened to make my stomach queasy. The worst that could happen is that I wouldn't have any useful information to add to the investigation.

Pip squeaked again, and I put the remainder of the scone in the bag with him.

I glanced up and noticed everyone staring at me expectantly. "Pip says he's ready to go."

"You'll have lunch with us here tomorrow. Be here at noon," Gladys said. It wasn't a request.

Officer Foster led me to the door. Outside the window, I noticed a silver sedan pass by. It reminded me about the man with the grabby hands. I turned back to the gossip club. "Do you ladies know a man with a scar on his cheek?" I demonstrated where the scar would be. "It's very pronounced."

Gladys and Emory shook their heads no. Allondra shrugged and said, "We know every soul in town, and we'd know a man with a scar. Why?"

I shook off my apprehension. "No reason."

Chapter Ten

Officer Foster lifted the yellow crime scene tape for me. I ducked under and sucked in a sharp breath as the ornate front door knocker sat at my nose level. He unlocked the door and pushed it open. I stepped inside and squished my bag so tight to my side that Pip made an oomph squirrel noise.

John Bleaker's house had held wonder and excitement for me the night before. Now all I could see were grim bluish-gray walls and trinkets that belonged to a man who would never again enjoy their beauty and significance.

I blinked hard and set my shoulders straight. I couldn't change what had happened, but I could help provide answers. Sherlock Holmes didn't let emotion cloud his powers of deduction and clue gathering. I rubbed my hands together and took in the living room. "Where did they find John's body?"

"Next to the coffee table in front of the television." He tiptoed around me. "Mind the crime scene dust. It gets everywhere."

The couch was in the same place as last night. Pillow cushions on the floor. Did that matter? The vase and flowers were no longer where Pip had spilled them the night before. Large sections of the carpet had been dissected and removed. All of this added up to… nothing. Absolutely nothing. I thought clues would jump out at me left and right, but I was no Sherlock Holmes.

After what seemed an eternity of silence, Officer Foster rested his hands on his police utility belt and let out a long sigh. "Shouldn't you be asking the squirrel what happened?"

Pip—my secret weapon. I lifted him out of the bag and held him in my palms. We couldn't communicate as we had the night before but maybe he could show me where to look if I asked the right questions. "Pip, does anything look out of place in the living room?"

He bounced out of my hands onto the couch, then the coffee table, and finally scurried up the post to his hanging cage. It swung from side to side as he sat on top of it, clinging to the top.

Then he leapt to the book case. The books I'd

fawned over were toppled to the side. Pip sat at the end of the books.

"One of the brick bookends is missing," I said. "It had little sailboats painted on it."

Officer Foster scribbled down the note. "Blunt force trauma is what county is saying how he died." He glanced up at me. "What else?"

I turned back to Pip. "What else?"

Pip jumped back to the top of his cage.

Officer Foster walked over and opened the front latch. Pip crawled inside and buried himself in the bedding, leaving only his tale showing above the pile.

"He's obviously very distraught over the loss of his owner," I said by way of an explanation.

"And you can't divine anything else helpful until he's properly rested or something like that?" His tone took on a sharp edge.

I shrugged. "Something like that."

"If the squirrel was here, then he would have seen the murderer. Can't you ask him who did it?"

"He didn't see the murder." I couldn't tell him how I knew that.

"That's convenient." Officer Foster closed his notebook and tucked it into his front pocket. "Nothing you've given me is useful."

The missing bookend must not have been the type of clue he needed.

"You know what I think? I think you're trying to point me in any direction that doesn't lead to your aunt." He stomped to the front door. "I think you've wasted enough of my time."

I removed Pip's cage from the hook and carried it to the front door. I hadn't meant to waste anyone's time, least of all a police officer searching for the truth. How was I to know I stunk at detecting until I'd given it a try? Motive, means, and opportunity were not my friends at the moment. Sadly, I didn't have many friends to count on in the human world. Yet.

Officer Foster waited for me on the front steps. After I passed through, he locked the door behind me. This time he didn't hold the crime scene tape. He passed under it and without another glance in my direction, got into his patrol car and backed it out onto the road. Then he drove away.

"I don't think he's the best Watson to my Holmes, anyway, Pip." I said it more to myself than the squirrel who slept so soundly he made little squeaky snores. He'd missed his safe place, cage or no cage. If my father were standing beside me, he'd say there was a lesson there somewhere for me to learn.

I would counter that in four days, I had a safe home to return to. The people of Lilac Cove still had a murderer at large.

A black SUV pulled into the drive across the road and Emory exited. She waved to me and I walked over. "How did it go?"

"Terrible."

"Did Officer Foster strand you here?"

I held up the cage. "I'm pretty sure I deserved it. Pip wasn't in the mood to help out with the investigation."

"I'm sure the little fella is exhausted. You can always try again when he's up for it." She nodded to her vehicle. "Climb in and I'll take you back to Fairyland Flowers. Word across the vines is that Chief Rayburn is bringing your Aunt Mossy home. I knew they didn't have enough to arrest her."

"Did the police interview you, since you live across the street? Did you notice anything unusual that night?" *Other than the weird family that appeared out of nowhere to ask what happened.*

"The county detective took a quick statement from all John's neighbors. I wear double hearing aids, which is why Olivia is able to keep sneaking out on me, so I wouldn't have heard anything coming from outside. I don't think anyone else did either. It's unnerving that something like that could happen so close to home and not any of us be aware of it."

I thought back to the man with the scar. If he

didn't live in the neighborhood, then why was he there at that time of night?

"Do you know if John had a lot of visitors?" I tapped the cage, going all in on my pet psychic lie. "According to Pip, he didn't have a lot of friends. Just the annoying ex-girlfriend that bossed him around."

"John liked to nose around in people's business, and that didn't make him a lot of friends." She gave me a quick smile. "There's an art to gossip, and John didn't have the flair my friends and I have for the give and take and sorting out the straight lies. We'll miss him just the same."

I wanted to hear more about the art of gossip but we'd already made it back to the town square. She pulled into the spot beside Mossy's car.

I turned toward her. "Aren't you scared that there's a killer in Lilac Cove?"

She leaned toward me as if to pass on a secret. "This was done by someone he knew. The only thing that scares me is that it'll take the police too long to figure it out."

"Thank you for the ride." I noticed the time on her dashboard as almost seven in the evening. My stomach rumbled as if knowing the numbers made a difference to how hungry I was.

Emory pulled out a pen and paper from her

center console. She scribbled down a phone number. "If you need anything at all, please call me."

"I appreciate all your help." I took the slip of paper and put it in my bag. Already the anxiety from a few minutes before receded. If I counted Emory, Olivia, and maybe Callan, I had made a few friends I could count on.

Mossy met me at the door to the flower shop. She swung it wide and beckoned me inside. "I've been worried. I thought you'd remain here until I returned."

"You've been worried? The police hauled you in for questioning and I didn't know that would take a full day."

She took Pip's cage from my hands. "No need to be alarmed. Chief Rayburn returned me safe and sound an hour ago. Are you hungry?"

"Starved, actually," I started. "But I want to know more about why the detective spent so long questioning you."

"It wasn't only me, my dear." She set Pip's cage down on her coffee table and busied herself with unwrapping sandwiches. "The mayor and her secretary came in for a statement too."

She put one in front of me. "It's a veggie delight with oil and vinegar. I think you'll like it."

"Aren't you going to eat?" I asked and took a

large bite of the sandwich. I moaned my satisfaction and closed my eyes. The flavors of cucumbers, tomatoes, and lettuce mixed together perfectly with the oil and vinegar.

She squeezed my shoulder. "I'm rather tired. I'd like to soak in the tub and then go straight to bed. I've made the sofa up for you with a pillow and blanket."

Mossy disappeared behind the sliding panel and soon the sound of water running filled the apartment.

Pip chittered from the coffee table, announcing the end of his nap. I brought him out of the cage and carried him to the table. When I offered him a good portion of the sandwich, he squeaked with delight.

"Me too, pal. Let's dig in."

By the time we finished the sandwich, and I cleared the table, Mossy stepped out from behind the screen and climbed into bed. She pulled a sleeping mask over her eyes and mumbled, "Goodnight, dear."

Moments later her snores shook her bed. I'd only ever heard my father make such a noise in his sleep.

Pip tilted his head to the side and then glanced at me before swishing his tail.

I shrugged. "I don't know how I'm going to sleep with that noise either."

I took the pajamas Mossy had laid out for me and changed behind the screen. I washed my face with a rag and used water from the tub. I'd take a proper bath in the morning, as I didn't want to make noise that could possibly wake my aunt. Although, with the noise she made, I wasn't sure that would be possible.

Unable to rest just yet, I bypassed the sofa and made my way into the flower shop. I'd noticed a few magazines on the counter earlier and thought reading might calm my racing mind. Why didn't Mossy want to tell me about what the detective asked her? Did she know something that she didn't want me to know?

I leaned on the counter and tapped my fingers on the edge. A shadow in the corner of the shop moved and my heart stalled before pounding so rapidly my chest shook.

Someone is in here with me. Had the real murderer come for me or Mossy? The image of the man with scar took hold of me and I couldn't let it go. Times like this were why I wish Dad had left me my wand. I reached beneath the counter and felt a pair of scissors.

I couldn't hurt a living creature. That most certainly was not my purpose. But maybe I could scare them enough so that they didn't hurt me.

The shadow moved again and then it shrunk. Shrinking shadows? I held the scissors up and called out, "Who's there?"

A flurry of wings came at me and darted around my head.

"Put those down, ninny!" The voice had yelled but at such a small size her command came out a high-pitched squeal.

"Iris." I put a hand over my chest willing my thundering heart to slow down. "What are you doing here?"

She landed on the counter and sat on a stapler. "I'm checking on my best friend."

"You almost gave me a heart attack."

"Aren't you glad to see me?" Her lips formed a pout.

"I am." I put the scissors on the counter and folded my arms, using them as a prop for my head. "How did you get out? Does my dad know you're here?"

"No way. And I can't stay long. When the rest of the fairies heard what happened, we all rushed to the fountain to watch. Some were even placing bets on how long it would take you to use your dust and return home."

"That's a little insulting." I wonder which way the bets were stacked.

"King Hypnum thought so, too. He's now banned all the fairy godparents from the fountain until after you return. It's driving your mom crazy. She snuck me out and asked me to stop by and check on you." She patted her hair and wiggled her eyebrows. "It's also driving Amaranth crazy."

"I'm actually doing great," I said, relieved that she nor any of the others would know the difference without the fountain. "I'm a vital part of the investigation."

"I knew giving you my FE was a terrible idea. This has turned into a disaster of epic proportions." Her flat tone told me she could see through my lie.

"But you're my best friend and you support me no matter what. Right?"

She tilted her head to the side and narrowed her eyes. "Are you going to ask me for something else that's going to get us both in trouble?"

"I need you to give me the ability to communicate with Pip again."

"The squirrel. That's the partner you need?"

"It's the best chance I have of getting the humans to take me seriously without telling them I'm a fairy. They assume I'm psychic and I let them run with the idea. I need to be able to communicate with Pip to make it work."

She huffed out a dramatic sigh but she'd already

withdrew her wand. "I don't know why I can't tell you no."

"Let me grab him. I'll be right back." I dashed into the apartment and snatched Pip from the cage where he'd once again curled under the bedding. He pressed his little body hard against my hands, searching to replace the warmth I'd stolen from him.

Back in the front flower shop, Iris used her wand to tap him on the head three times. "Talk."

"Wait," I stopped her. "Be specific, just in case. I can't have him talking to everyone."

"Fine." She tapped his head three times again. "Talk to Juniper only about super important things."

Pip rolled over in my hands and went back to sleep. My questions would wait until the morning anyway. Wouldn't he be surprised when he realized he could talk again?

Iris flitted into the air. She flew close to my face and gave me a kiss on the cheek. "Stay safe. There are some bad people in Lilac Cove."

I narrowed my eyes. "Have you seen who the killer is through the fountain?"

She shook her head, but her violet eyes clouded. "I haven't, but I've never seen your father so distraught, Juniper. He knows more than he lets on to the rest of us."

He could be here, helping me instead of

watching me flounder, I wanted to say. As angry as I might be with Dad, I still wouldn't disrespect him, even in front of Iris. "Don't worry. I'll see you all in four days."

"Believe it or not, the majority of us are rooting for you." Iris tapped her head three times. "Home."

In a poof, she was gone. At least now I knew the bets were stacked in my favor.

Chapter Eleven

Sleep didn't come easy on the sofa, and as soon as Mossy's feet hit the floor, I snatched the blanket away and met her in the kitchen.

"Tea, my dear?" she asked.

I stood close enough to invade her personal space. "Yes, please. But we need to talk."

She placed a hand over her mouth and let out a wide yawn. "What about?"

"John Bleaker."

Mossy set two teacups on the counter and, after a moment of contemplation, turned to me. "What happened to John is a tragedy. I'm sad he's gone, and I'm sad to have lost a one-time friend. But there's nothing you can do that the police aren't already doing."

"I need to help them."

"No, you don't." Her tone took on a sternness that rivaled my dad's. "That's not how things work in the human world. Bad things happen and there is no one to wave a wand or sprinkle fairy dust to fix it."

I backed up a step. I'd thought Mossy to be my ally.

She turned her attention back to fixing the tea. She filled each cup with water from the tap and placed them in the microwave to warm them for a minute.

After placing a tea bag in my cup, she set it in front of me. Then she smiled as if everything were settled.

"I have a meeting with the mayor this morning to go over the final flower arrangements for the festival Friday night. I'm so glad you'll still be here for the festival. It's the highlight of the year for Lilac Cove."

The mayor. John's place of employment, and the next stop on my list. *Sorry, Mossy, but I won't let this go. Not until I fix it.*

"Can I go with you to your meeting?" I asked.

She lifted one shoulder in a half-shrug. "I don't see why not. We have about an hour to get ready."

Pip rustled around in his cage and emitted a series of chitters. Mossy disappeared behind the screen, and I took the opportunity to have a quick conversation with my partner.

I opened the cage and he hopped on the front of my pajamas.

"Pip, can you understand me?"

He gave a little nod.

"Try saying something to me to see if I can understand you."

"I'm hungry," he squeaked out.

I rubbed a finger over his head. "Perfect."

He crawled to my shoulder. "We can communicate again? I thought that other fairy was a part of a dream."

"We can, but we'll have to be sly about it. No one else can understand you, but I'll have to be careful not to draw too much attention to myself when we're together."

"I'm still hungry," he said.

I took that as an acknowledgement and searched through Mossy's refrigerator for something he could nibble on. With the way Mossy used the microwave to heat water and the fact that her fridge stood empty, I guessed she didn't enjoy cooking. I found a box of microwave waffles in the freezer. *Better than nothing.* At least she had a toaster.

A minute later, I broke apart the crispy toasted waffle for Pip. At first he nibbled, then put large pieces inside his mouth to puff up his cheeks. He mumbled something at me.

"I can't understand you with your mouth full."

He mumbled it again and a piece of waffle fell out of his mouth, but I still didn't catch what he said. Mossy came out from behind the screen. Distracted by her presence, he jumped from the table to the sofa to the bed and back toward his cage.

"Bouncy little thing, isn't he? I don't remember him being so energetic at John's house. What are you going to do with him when you leave?" Mossy wore a deep purple shirt and when she turned her back to pull a pair of shoes from under the bed, I saw that she had painted glittery fairy wings on the back of it.

Pip stood on his hind legs on the coffee table and waited for me to answer her. He blinked rapidly.

"I hadn't thought that far ahead, but I guess he can come live with me in the palace, if he wants."

Another piece of waffle fell out of his mouth.

Mossy laughed, the sound light and airy. "Your father is going to love that."

"Dad will adjust."

She eyed me, a smile playing at her lips. "Get ready, my dear. We don't want to be late."

After a quick bath, I borrowed another flowery dress from Mossy. I paired it with the blue shoes again. They'd worked well enough yesterday. The mirror above the sink showed what a disaster my hair had become. I worked it into a thick French braid and let the tail fall down the middle of my back.

My mind worked ahead on the information I'd need to acquire from our time in the mayor's office. Did I ask pointed questions and risk being asked to leave? If I played it safe and only observed, then I might miss the opportunity to further my investigation. I pulled my fairy pouch from my bag. I could sprinkle the tiniest amount of dust on my head for luck.

"Juniper, let's go, dear."

I put the pouch back in the bag. *Last resort, remember?* I pushed back the screen and walked over to put Pip in the bag.

"Dear, why don't you leave him here? We're going to a professional meeting, and I don't want the little guy to cause a distraction."

Leave my talking squirrel partner behind? I couldn't form an argument that made sense so I conceded and closed Pip inside his cage. "I'll bring you back a big lunch, okay?"

He shook his head up and down but cut his eyes at Mossy.

"We aren't far from the city hall so we won't need to drive," she said.

I took one last glance at Pip and followed her out the door. I'd come back for him later.

Once outside, the morning sun hit my face with a blast of warmth.

We cut across a park with benches and a fenced in area for walking dogs. Allondra sat in a fold out chair while a black and tan Doberman danced around her. They were the only two in the dog park and when she noticed us, she waved and shouted, "Morning y'all!"

I waved back but stayed away from the fence when her dog stuck his long snout through a fence hole to get a better whiff of us.

"I heard you met Allondra and Emory and Gladys yesterday at the café. They really are the loveliest of women, but beware, as they like to spread gossip and matchmake."

"Matchmake?"

"Pair up single women with the single men in town."

Nothing I had to worry about.

"Which reminds me. Are you betrothed?"

"Not yet." I toyed with the straps on my bag. "The captain of the guard and I have courted, I guess you could call it."

"Ooh, captain of the guard. Not a handsome fairy prince from the north?"

"I might surprise everyone and rule without marrying."

Mossy stumbled over a chunk of uprooted grass. She grabbed my arm for support and busted into a rancorous laughter that boarded on hysterical. "My, my. The fairy monarchy has changed quite a bit since I left."

"What do you mean?"

"Has your father never told you?" She leaned forward and checked my expression carefully. "I'm the eldest, not Hypnum. I gave up the right to ascend to the throne because I wouldn't marry a prince from the Scottish isles of fairies."

She shook her head and let go of my arm. I followed behind her a little slower than before, the news of what she'd given up sinking in. Mossy, the rightful queen of our fairy godparent kingdom? Why would Dad hide something like that from me? Had he kept me locked up from the human world for fear that I'd do the same?

Mossy stopped short in front of a door that led into a two-story building. The boxy font on the glass window said *Lilac Cove City Hall.*

Mossy smoothed the top of her hair, but her easy smile had been replaced with a frown. The door remained locked and she pressed a button on the side.

"Yes?" the voice from the speaker box squawked at us.

Mossy leaned toward the box. "Mossy here to see Mayor Caldwell. She's expecting us."

A loud buzzer announced the door had been unlocked. Mossy held it open for me as I passed through. The bottom half of the building remained dark. A row of chairs sat in front of a counter with a sign that reminded everyone that they didn't open until ten a.m.

"This way," Mossy said. She took me to an elevator and we waited while whatever happened behind the closed metal doors made the most horrific screeching sound.

"Can't we take the stairs?" I pointed to the stairwell. I didn't anticipate that the ride in anything that made retching noises could be considered safe.

"All these old buildings sound scary. We'll be fine."

I noticed that for the third or fourth time she'd spoken to me, she hadn't used a "my dear" or "dear" after.

We rode up in silence. I debated on whether or not to further the conversation about her banishment. I didn't have much time with my aunt and leaving on an uncomfortable note would tarnish our reunion. I'd speak to her again in the evening. For now, I'd put all my focus on finding John's killer.

The elevator doors opened to a brunette with a

sleek bob stomping her foot outside her office. "Why won't the password work, Brianna? It's the same password I've used for two years."

"I don't know, *Mayor*." Brianna spit back at her. "John set up all the administrative stuff for our laptops and he had them all in his office for updates a couple of days ago. We'll have to call someone in to help."

"You're the secretary. Be a real secretary for a change and do your job." Mayor Caldwell glanced up and noticed us watching her tirade. She smoothed down the front of her emerald green dress suit. "Ladies, welcome. Brianna didn't tell me you were here already."

Brianna shrugged. "I didn't get a chance because you wouldn't stop yelling."

The mayor cut her a look that promised more of the yelling later. She strode over to us, her black three-inch high heels clicking across the tile floor.

Now those were shoes that would make everyone take a person seriously. I needed to check my aunt's stash to see if she had any like those.

She stuck out her hand. "I don't believe we've met. I'm Nicole Caldwell. Mayor of our little slice of heaven."

I grasped her hand and when she squeezed hard enough to make me flinch, I snatched it back. "I'm

Juniper. Mossy's niece."

After a full once over, she turned her attention to Mossy.

"As you can tell, I'm lost at sea without John." She pulled Mossy into a faux hug, the kind where there was no real warmth or comfort intended. "And with that, I'm afraid I have more bad news."

"How so?" Mossy asked pulling away from her.

"You'll have to see for yourself." Mayor Caldwell led the way into her expansive office. The stark office was absent of color and warmth and it matched her in style so perfectly, I couldn't imagine anyone else ever occupying the same space. She picked up a stack of yellow slips of paper from her desk and waved them at us.

"What are those?" I asked.

"Invoices." Mossy supplied.

"Falsified invoices." She slapped them down on the desk. "Thousands of dollars in flowers bought from Fairyland Flowers, if it's even possible to spend that much in your little shop."

Mossy reached across the desk. "That's ridiculous. I have never invoiced for more than the weekly arrangements and the festival each year. That's a few hundred at the most."

"Well, if you didn't do it, someone did. It's been happening for the past two years and all paid in petty cash."

Mossy flipped through the pieces of paper. "This isn't my handwriting. And I think I'd know how to properly spell peonies. One 'e,' not two."

"Briana and I agree that it might be John's." She pressed a hand to her chest as if saying the words out loud pained her.

"What is a petty cash?" I asked, noting Mossy's distress but unsure how to help.

"An amount of cash taken out weekly so that checks don't have to be constantly waiting on my desk for a signature. John handled all of it."

Mossy sunk into a brown leather chair. She laid the invoices back on the desk near an ornate paperweight in the shape of a squirrel. It reminded me of Pip, and I wondered if he would know anything about the false invoices.

Mossy waved her hand toward the stack of yellow paper. "You think John wrote false invoices from my store and stole the cash? John was nosy to a fault, but he wasn't a thief."

"The only other plausible explanation would be that you wrote those invoices and collected that cash."

Mossy stiffened.

Mayor Caldwell leaned forward. "Until we can get this mishandling of city funds investigated properly by the police department, I'm afraid we won't be using your services for the festival on Friday."

Mossy pushed forward in the chair. "That's my biggest order of the year."

"What if the police can prove that Mossy wasn't involved with the petty cash? Would that make it possible for her to provide the arrangements for Friday?" I asked.

Mayor Caldwell narrowed her eyes. "I've never seen our police department move that quickly."

"What if I can prove it?" I challenged her. In the two days I'd been in town, Mossy had lost her friend and her business was in danger. I couldn't take away her throne and watch her suffer in the human world too. Since I'd already made John my main focus, adding the petty cash mystery to the pile didn't seem like that much more to handle.

I had an ace in my pocket in that Pip could now speak and give me more information.

"If you think you can resolve this faster, then by all means, be my guest."

Mossy stood. "I need to open Fairyland. I appreciate you bringing this to my attention, Mayor." She nodded to the elevator. "Let's go, Juniper."

We passed by Brianna who pretended to click away at the laptop, but I could tell from the sailboat on her login screen she wasn't actually doing any work. I hovered near her but she picked up her desk phone and pretended not to see me.

I'd needed to question her about John and their relationship, but instead I'd added an additional mystery and I was quickly running out of days to solve them both.

Chapter Twelve

Once outside of city hall, I stopped Mossy by grabbing her forearm and giving it a gentle squeeze. "I'm sure that was upsetting to hear about John. Are you sure he couldn't have taken the money?"

She turned to me, the events from upstairs taking a toll on her expression. "John didn't need to steal from his job. Not many people know this, but he lived off of a sizeable inheritance from an uncle who passed several years ago. He could have quit any time he wanted, but he liked being at the hub of everything that happened in Lilac Cove. It doesn't make sense."

It didn't. Especially since Pip said John was about to lose his house because of money missing from his account. Where did all the money go? I wanted to ask Mossy more about John's financial situation but I could tell she was upset over being accused of writing up the fake invoices.

"Who else would have access to your invoices?" I asked.

"Anyone who wandered in the store, I guess. I don't lock it when I make deliveries around town because I don't keep enough cash on hand for anyone to steal. I never thought the blank invoices would be taken. Nothing like this has happened before."

"If John were in charge of petty cash, would he be the one who paid the invoices?"

Mossy put the palm of her hand against her forehead. "I'm getting a bit of a headache thinking about it. I know you want to help with this too, but I'd prefer you not get involved. The mayor can let Chief Rayburn handle it. You really shouldn't have offered to clear my name."

I tilted my head and offered her a small smile. "Isn't that what family do for each other?"

She cast her gaze down at the sidewalk and it hit me that she'd come into the human world with nothing and no help from family and had made it on her own. I understood her reluctance to ask for help now after all these years. Not wanting to add additional stress to her day, I nudged her with my shoulder.

"I'll help you open the flower shop and promise to stay out of your hair the rest of the day."

We started down the sidewalk and linked our arms. With every step, Mossy's spine straightened a little more. "What are you going to do to pass the time, my dear?"

"I've made a couple of friends in town. I think I'll pay them a visit."

"Do you mean Callan?" she said and winked.

I tucked in my lips. As far as human men went, he was attractive, yet something about his withdrawn nature warned me he had some unresolved issues in his past. Plus, the whole issue of I'm a fairy godparent and he's a human made it impossible to even consider flirting.

"Actually, Emory and the other gossip ladies invited me for lunch at the café. I think I'll take them up on their offer. Before that, maybe I'll finish taking a tour around Lilac Cove. I want to soak up as much as I can before my five days of living as a human are up."

I dropped Mossy off at the front door to the flower shop and decided against grabbing Pip just yet. I wanted to double back to city hall and ask the mayor for a copy of one of the invoices. If I could start putting together a timeline of when the invoices were submitted, not to mention get the handwriting sampling, then I'd have a good place to start.

I gave myself a mental pat on the back. I almost sounded like a real Sherlock Holmes.

City Hall didn't officially open for another thirty minutes and this time when I pressed the buzzer, no one answered. I knocked on the front door but didn't see anyone at the counter. Every building had a back door. I'd try my luck with that.

Most of the buildings making up the square were connected, and I had to walk back down to the corner to find an opening to get into the alley behind them. A turn-in led me to a row of rusty dumpsters, each back door having one sitting beside it. City Hall sat on the corner so it wouldn't be too hard for me to find which door belonged to it. I passed the back of the café where the gossip club had shared information the day before. The smell of fresh baked bread wafted out from the cracks. I looked forward to lunch and getting more information.

Three doors away from my target, a heated argument caught my attention. I recognized the mayor immediately but the man she argued with had his back turned. Investigators have to eavesdrop, I told myself. To stay out of sight, I slid behind a dumpster, careful to keep the majority of my body hidden.

Still too far back to hear their exact words, a spike of adrenaline rushed through me when the man backed Mayor Caldwell against the wall and grabbed her wrist. *Not on my watch.*

"Hey!" I shouted and came out from my hiding place.

The man turned toward me and his angry face transformed into a wild smile. I recognized him as the man picking up keys from the police station on the first night. "Vinnie?"

He stepped away from the mayor. "How nice to see you again, Juniper. How's your visit in Lilac Cove."

I ignored his question. The smile didn't erase the fact he'd been forceful with the mayor. "What's going on?"

"My Air B&B isn't up to standard and the mayor and I were having a disagreement about the return of my deposit."

Mayor Caldwell rubbed her wrist. "That's right. It got a little heated but it's no big deal." She addressed the man. "I'll have your money before you check out on Friday."

"I guess that will have to do," he said and turned to me. "Nice to see you again."

The mayor and I watched him walk to the end of the alley and disappear around the corner.

"Are you okay?" I asked. "I thought the police chief owned the B&B thing?"

"It's really none of your concern," she snapped and raked her cold gaze over me. "What do you want? Have you solved the invoice situation already?"

"I was hoping to look through the invoices again and maybe take some notes."

She let out an annoyed sigh and her gaze darted to the end of the alley again before landing on me. "I'll have Brianna make copies for you and send them around to Fairyland Flowers this afternoon."

"Not to the flower shop," I said in a rush of words. "Have them sent over around noon to the café." When she furrowed her brow, I quickly added, "I don't want to worry Mossy with them any more than she already is."

Mayor Caldwell shrugged. "Whatever."

When I didn't move to leave she narrowed her eyes. "Anything else?"

Honestly, the mayor intimidated me and I didn't want to outright ask her about her alibi. While I didn't feel in danger being alone with her, I had a feeling she could make things very difficult for Mossy when I left if I pushed her too hard. However, when Brianna brought the invoices over, I'd ask her about their alibi instead. Out of the two, I thought Brianna to be the weakest link.

"No. I'm good," I said.

She turned her back to me and used a keycard to enter the back door. She shut it hard in my face and I headed back to the end of the alley where I'd come in.

I strolled across the park and sat down on one of the benches outside the dog area. Allondra and her dog were gone and I had the place to myself. Good. I needed to think. All of this information gathering meant nothing if I couldn't figure a way to put it in order. I'd been to the crime scene but Pip couldn't help me. Doubtful I'd convince Officer Foster or the Chief to allow me in again. John's place of work, City Hall, turned up more trouble than answers.

That left me with significant others. They'd cleared Mossy but I couldn't help the suspicion she hid something from me. I needed to know more about Brianna. That could be helped with the gossip club at noon as long as I could provide them with some valuable information to trade.

"You're thinking hard."

I startled as Callan sat beside me.

"I'm sorry," he said. "I didn't mean to scare you."

"Actually, I'm so glad you're here," I said.

"Really?"

"Did you come from the police station?"

"Yes, but I have the next four nights off so I'm not going to sleep this morning in order to give me a little internal clock reset." He quirked an eyebrow. "I'm free all day."

"Perfect. I need to pick your detective brain some more."

"Not this again." He crossed his arms and sat back with a huff. "I'm not a detective anymore. Plus, from what I heard last night from the chief, Mrs. M has been cleared as a suspect."

"The killer is still out there." I gestured to the building in front of us. "I caught the mayor arguing with a man in the alley. There's a man with a scar following me around. Something's not right in Lilac Cove."

"You're going to turn into one of the gossip club women if you don't watch out."

"I meet with them at noon."

He uncrossed his arms and turned toward me, his face taking on the expression he'd used when scolding Olivia. "No good ever comes from amateur snoops interfering with a police investigation. The way it works is that you pass on what you know and take a step back."

"I don't mean to interfere, but I can't take a step back. I have to help find John's killer," I argued.

"I can't be the one to help you." He stood and

wiped a hand across his brow.

"Fine," I said.

"Fine," he repeated and walked away, his shoulders squared.

I took a deep steadying breath. I didn't need the moody man's assistance.

I had a talking squirrel. One who may or may not have an attention span problem, but still *a talking squirrel.*

Chapter Thirteen

Fairyland Flowers only had one customer. The man with the scar. He pretended he didn't see me when I flew through the shop door, and I stopped short at the counter, keeping him within my peripheral vision.

Mossy busied herself with picking wilted flowers out of a bin of carnations. She smiled as I sidled up beside her.

"Do you know that man?" I whispered.

Her eyes flickered in his direction. "No, but he's the first customer I've had all morning. It would appear that the mayor has let it slip that I might be stealing funds from the festival. I've had three phone calls with canceled orders already this morning."

"How awful."

"It'll blow over, and Chief Rayburn has

promised to get to the bottom of it all. But he's busy, so I may have to deep discount my inventory and try selling roses one by one out in the park." She shrugged. "Wouldn't be the first time."

I gave her side hug. "I'm going to fix this. At my lunch with the gossip club, I'll have them reverse the gossip started by the mayor."

She used her free hand to boop the end of my nose. Then she broke off the stem from a carnation and slipped it behind my ear. "You're a good niece. I wish I had you around more."

"Me too." Maybe Dad would let me visit now that I've spent a few days in his crash course living as the humans. "I'm off to see Pip, but I'll check back with you soon. Don't despair."

The man with the scar scratched under his nose and, after standing in front of a fern for much longer than necessary, walked out the door without buying anything. I may be naïve about a lot of things in the human world, but I knew when someone spied. What I couldn't figure out is how he connected to John Bleaker. Pip might know, though.

I rushed to the back to grab Pip's cage. He squeaked and chittered and flicked his tail in every direction. "Hi, Pip. I need you to identify someone for me. We have to hurry before he gets down the sidewalk."

I reached for the top of the cage and that's when I noticed the note. *No cheating. Sincerely, Dad.* The note crumpled away when I picked it off the cage. What did he mean *cheating?* "Pip?"

Pip chittered. "Pip, Pip."

Oh no. My one secret advantage. "Please say something other than your name."

He jumped around inside the cage and flicked his tail three more times. "Pip, Pip. Hungry."

"Anything other than your name and hungry?"

"Pip, Pip. Hungry," he said and gave the squirrel equivalent of a shrug.

Dad took away our ability to communicate. Again.

"That wasn't cheating!" I yelled into the air just in case Dad watched me from the courtyard fountain. Of course he watched. That was the only way he could know that Iris had been there and helped.

I needed Pip to talk.

I opened the cage door and Pip jumped onto the front of my dress. Back out in the main shop area, the door jingled when a man passed through.

"Hello, Mossy-girl. How's business?" The tall man with brown hair and a neatly trimmed goatee sauntered to the counter.

"Terrible, thanks to your wife," Mossy answered.

"She can be a handful, can't she?" He leaned on

the counter and flashed bright white teeth at the both of us. "Regardless, I need my usual order today. Two dozen red roses, with one white rose in the middle."

"White is the symbol of true love," I offered even though no one had asked.

Mossy snorted but quickly composed herself when the man shot her a dark look. She nodded toward me. "This is my niece, Juniper. Juniper, this is the mayor's husband, Dr. Caldwell."

He winked at me and gestured at the flowers. "Can you have them delivered? I'm afraid I have patients waiting at the office."

"I'll take them," I offered. The faster I got the copy of invoices from Brianna and proved Mossy had nothing to do with stealing the funds, the faster I'd see a smile return to her face.

"I'll have them ready before the end of the hour," Mossy said.

He nodded to her and tossed a credit card on the counter.

While she rang up his charges, he turned his smile to me. "I hope you're settling in to our little town just fine."

"Other than the murder and false accusations of my aunt stealing, it's turning out to be a great visit," I said.

He didn't flinch. "If you need someone to show

you around, I'd be happy to stop by this evening. We have some hidden spots down by the beach."

I blinked hard. Was the mayor's husband offering to take me to a secluded beach area, just the two of us?

Pip barked at him.

Mossy cleared her throat. "Do you need a receipt?"

"Think about it," he said to me before turning back to her. "I'm good. See you around Mossy-girl."

He covered his eyes with dark sunglasses and strolled to the exit.

I shivered and rubbed my arms.

Mossy waited for the door to close all the way before saying, "Stay away from that one."

"I plan to," I assured her. Pip took a few more hops and landed near my shoulder. Then he fussed with my braid as if he had a nut he wanted to hide in the interlocked hair. "Pip, Pip. Hungry."

Mossy snapped her fingers and Pip jumped onto the counter. She pulled a sleeve of crackers from beneath the counter and opened them for him. Pip chittered with delight.

"Wait," I started. "Did you understand Pip just now?"

"I'm starting to recognize his hungry grunts, if that's what you mean." She shrugged off my question and fixed the vase with the red roses and baby's breath. When it came to the white rose, she wrinkled her nose in distaste.

"Do you doubt his love for his wife?" I asked, sensing between the expression and her snort earlier, she knew something about his marital status.

"I doubt that man's love for anyone," she replied. "But it's not our business. Thank you for delivering the flowers. I'll keep Pip here since I'm not busy. I'll return him to his cage when he gets tired, or if he causes too much trouble."

I rubbed a finger over his tiny head. "You won't cause any trouble, will you?"

His tail flickered twice which I took to mean "yes." *Take that, Dad. We can still somewhat communicate.*

The vase took both hands and Mossy had to let me out the door. I checked left and right, craning my neck over the roses, but didn't see the scar man. How did he disappear so quickly?

I trudged the path back to city hall for the third time that morning. Now that it was open, I didn't need to ring the buzzer, but I had to wait for someone to open the door for me. The lobby had two or three people occupying the plastic chairs while a woman with thick eyebrows sat at the counter. At the elevator, I used my foot to press the up arrow.

Elevator music filtered in from a speaker above my head as I rode up to the second floor. This time when I approached Brianna, she didn't pretend to be on the phone.

She gasped at the flowers. "Are those from Dr. Caldwell?"

The mayor's door was closed and I could hear her bark at someone from the other side. I had to be fast with my questions for Brianna. I set the flowers on the end of the desk. "They're for the mayor."

She sniffed the bouquet, a red blush creeping up her tan neck. "Of course they are."

"The mayor was going to have you copy the fake invoices for me. I can grab them now if you have a minute so you don't have to deliver them to the café."

She pulled out the white rose and set it aside. She cut her eyes at me. "What invoices?"

"The fake ones that my aunt is accused of sending over to John for flower arrangements never delivered."

She shrugged. "The mayor hasn't said anything to me."

"But you were here earlier during the meeting with my aunt. I saw you eavesdropping."

"The mayor hasn't given me anything," she repeated and pointed to a tray labeled *in box*. The box had so many papers sitting on top that it spilled to the side of her desk. How would she know the difference? The mayor and her secretary were making things ten times harder than they needed to be. No wonder John had been looking for another job. The reminder of the interview that he'd never made it to because of me spurred on my determination. Brianna had to know something about his leaving.

"Did you know John Bleaker was leaving as deputy mayor?"

She sat back and let out a laugh that sounded like a baby goat choking. "John would never leave the mayor's office. It held too much power for him. Always having an inside peak into everyone's business."

"It's true," I said. "He was."

She sobered and her face took on a hard edge, scarier than the mayor's had been in the alley way. "Just who are you? You've been in town for exactly two minutes and you're in everyone's business already. Stop spending time with those gossip hags. You didn't know John and you don't know me. So go back to your little fairy flower shop and mind your own business."

I'd underestimated her, it seemed. She was as strong a link as the mayor. I gave up on getting any useful information from her and headed back to the elevator.

While I waited, I watched Brianna and tried to get a read on her. It seemed that as soon as I'd walked away it was if Brianna had forgotten all about me. She turned her attention to the white rose. She rubbed the petals against her cheek and smiled. If I didn't know any better, I'd suspect she thought that white rose was meant for her.

Chapter Fourteen

I sat inside the café for an hour before the gossip club showed up for our lunch date. Emory, Allondra, and Gladys walked in together, two of the three with huge smiles. Gladys wore the frown.

"We know what we're doing for our May Day Festival booth Friday night," Emory said.

"What's a May Day booth?" I asked.

"Usually, we sell our canned goods. Tomatoes, fig preserves, and sweet pickles." Gladys sat down and crossed her arms.

"That's so last year," Allondra said. "This year we're going to have a pet psychic tent."

Uh oh.

"That's right," Emory said on peal of laughter. "You're going to talk to people's pets. We'll charge five dollars a chat. That's more than we were charging per can of our best preserves."

How did I tell them that I couldn't talk to animals? Not even Pip. "I don't think that's a good idea. My psychic powers don't work on command. In fact, what happened with John's squirrel could be considered a fluke."

"Told you," Gladys said and finally smiled. "We'll keep to the canned goods this year."

Emory sat back and pursed her lips.

Allondra wasn't one to give up so easily. "This morning when Killer sniffed you through the fence, he didn't try to bite anyone all day long. I think your powers are working just fine."

I put my hand out. "Why don't we table this discussion and we'll come back to it later. I actually need some more information from you ladies."

The atmosphere around them changed. I knew the game. Give a lot to get a lot. I only hope I had enough to give.

"John had an interview set for yesterday morning. Do any of you know why he would leave the mayor's office?"

Gladys played with the cloth napkin in front of her. "He was always threatening to leave the mayor high and dry. But he never made good on it."

Allondra leaned in but didn't lower her voice. "I heard he once wrote a three-page resignation letter."

"It's because of that Brianna," Emory added.

"She was dating both him and a certain married man at the same time. She's attracted to money. Always has been."

The table quieted and I plunged forward with another tidbit to feed their gossip monsters. "Dr. Caldwell sent roses to the mayor's office today. Brianna pulled out a single white one among the red and acted like she'd been expecting it."

Emory slapped the top of the table. "I knew it. When Dr. Caldwell and John had a tiff in front of John's house last month, I knew the talk about him and Brianna had to be true. I think John threatened to tell Mayor Caldwell."

"Did he?" I asked. "Do you think the police have questioned Dr. Caldwell about the murder?"

Gladys sipped her tea, then leaned forward. "Officer Foster said that the mayor, Dr. Caldwell, and Brianna all gave each other strong alibis. While it seems fishy, I doubt the three of them would be in on it together."

The women shrugged. Allondra sat back and gave her a wink. "You should ask Callan what he hears down at the station more about it. You two seemed awful cozy on the park bench earlier today."

I glanced at Emory and Gladys who had both leaned in anticipating my answer. Their attention span was worse than Pip's.

I rested my chin on my hands. "Callan is very nice, but he refuses to help me with the investigation into John's death. And that's what I need right now."

Gladys tsked. "That's because of what happened in Atlanta."

"What happened in Atlanta?" I sat in awe of how easily she'd turned my focus.

She tapped her fingers on the table. "It was all part of a big raid on some mobster thugs running guns. He arrested a very bad man and one of the underlings capped his partner. All he does now is run the dispatch and take care of Olivia."

Poor Callan.

"Anyway," Allondra began. "What do you think about our pet psychic idea? You can make stuff up and it will still bring in a crowd. Everyone in town is convinced you can talk to the squirrel."

I eyed her and hid my smile. "I wonder who gave them that idea in the first place?"

"Officer Foster," Emory said flatly. "I hate how that man beats us to the good stuff sometimes."

They'd given me so much information that I didn't want to disappoint them. I could pretend to talk to animals for a couple of hours. "If I'm still in town by Friday night, then I will sit in your tent and talk to the animals."

Emory slapped the top of the table again.

Allondra clapped her hands. Gladys frowned.

"We'll take care of everything," Allondra said. "All you have to do is show up."

We ordered our sandwiches and after enjoying the quick meal together, said our goodbyes. I walked back to Fairyland Flowers with a plan forming. If John had in fact written a three-page resignation letter, then I could almost bet it'd be in that tray on Brianna's desk and she wouldn't know for months.

If I could get in and find it, I might be able to see if he'd mentioned any other secrets than the one about Brianna and Dr. Caldwell sneaking around behind the mayor's back.

Chapter Fifteen

Once again, Mossy went to bed early and within minutes snored like an angry animal fighting another angry animal over its dinner. I'd spent the afternoon hanging around the flower shop and preparing my outfit for the night's excursion. From her closet I'd borrowed the perfect black shirt and pants along with black tennis shoes. I'd also found a black scarf and I wrapped it around my head to cover my hair. I'd found a flashlight under the sink.

Fairies often poofed in and out of places undetected, so I didn't consider my plan an act of breaking and entering.

I held my pouch of fairy dust against my chest. I'd use just a little to get the electronic door to open at the mayor's office. The rest would be kept for an extreme emergency.

The back door gave a creak as I opened it, but the sound only caused Mossy to roll over on her side. Interesting enough, that position stopped the snoring.

I walked the length of the alley when a rustling caught my attention. *Please don't be the scarred man.*

Olivia jumped out of the shadows and shouted, "Hey."

I yelped and grabbed my chest. "What are you doing out here so late?"

She glanced at her wristwatch. "It's only ten, and I am fourteen."

"You're grounded," I reminded her.

"Yeah, but this is Uncle Callan's first night off and when he stays up all day, he crashes pretty early. He won't even know I'm missing. Plus, I wanted to come say hello and see how your investigation is going."

"What investigation?" I asked.

Her gaze started at my head and traveled to my toes and back. "Why are you dressed like a ninja? Are you going spying? Can I come?"

"Absolutely not." I pointed to her bicycle she'd tossed haphazardly on the ground. "You're going to ride back home now or I'm going to call your uncle."

"Rude," she said, the hurt showing in her sour expression. "I only want to help."

"I'm not spying. I'm on my way back to the flower shop." I turned and pretended to take a few steps in the direction from where I'd come. "Nothing to see here."

"Right," she said. "Fine. Bye."

She hovered near her bike and watched me, so I turned my back to her. I walked all the way to Mossy's back door and stood there counting to fifty. I didn't want to risk waking my aunt by going inside so I ducked down in the shadows just in case Olivia hung around to test my lie.

I tiptoed down to the corner and checked in every direction. No Olivia. Good. She'd gone home like she'd been told.

Mossy had told me earlier that she was the only storekeeper who lived behind her shop. All the other stores closed down around six p.m., and then the square became deserted. I found this to be true as I didn't pass another person as I cut through the park and into the back alley of city hall.

The alley behind city hall had become the thing nightmares are made of. I wasn't usually scared of the dark, but I didn't want to use the flashlight just yet. The one security light attached to a tall pole flickered on and off and the moon hadn't been kind enough to grant enough light for me to see clearly.

My walk down the alley took forever. I passed a

dumpster and a raccoon poked out his head. I held a finger to my lips to shush him. He glared at me and then returned to whatever waited for him in the trash. At least I wasn't completely alone.

Before using my coveted supply of fairy dust on the door, I tried the knob thinking maybe it would be left open. No such luck. I pinched the smallest amount of dust between my thumb and pointer finger and sprinkled it on the doorknob.

The door opened with ease and I stepped inside and waited for an alarm. If it went off, then I'd have to use dust on the control system, too. The little light on the box stayed green and I wondered if the last person out had forgotten to set it.

I bypassed the elevator and used the emergency exit stairs to the second floor. So far, so good. I started at Brianna's desk and held the flashlight high over the pile of papers spilling from her inbox. One by one I carefully set them aside in order. Not that I think she'd notice if I messed them up. Most of the pieces of paper were invoices and second and third notices. Some as far back as a month or two. I thought the mayor said John handled the invoices? Maybe that was only for petty cash. Or maybe he hadn't been paying any bills and keeping all the petty cash for himself. That didn't make sense with what Mossy had said about his inheritance.

"What are we searching for?" Olivia appeared beside me.

I screamed and slapped my hand over my mouth. After three deep breaths, I narrowed my eyes. "What are you doing here? I told you to go home. Your uncle will kill us both."

"I followed you like a true spy." She smiled and took the flashlight from me. "You left the door unlocked, but don't worry, I hit the star button on the keypad and locked it behind us. Tell me what we're searching for so we can work faster."

I gritted my teeth. At least if I kept an eye on her in here, I could walk her home right after. "Allondra mentioned a possible resignation letter full of secrets from John. I need to find if it exists, and if the mayor or Brianna kept a copy."

"Did you check John's old office?" she asked.

I glanced around. "I didn't even notice that he had one."

"It's around the corner in an old broom closet. He used to complain to Emory about it all the time."

We walked past the mayor's office to the corner of the building and found a closed door. A nameplate had once been attached to the wall but now all that remained was a sticky residue. Inside sat a desk with a rolling chair behind it. Drawers on the desk had been left half-open and papers were scattered to the floor.

"Looks like someone already searched through it," I said.

Olivia held the flashlight. "It could have been the police. They're awful messy when they search things. I heard Officer Foster tell Uncle Callan that the sheriff's office couldn't find John's work laptop."

I knew for a fact that his laptop was on his coffee table in his house that night. I could pass that information on to Officer Foster but I doubt he'd trust me again after I didn't provide anything useful at the crime scene.

Olivia clicked off the flashlight.

"I can't see," I said, trying to hold a piece of paper up to the window.

"Shh. I hear someone."

I dropped the paper on the desk and rushed to her. We clamped on to each other. I tilted my head to the side and heard the ding of the elevator.

"We have to get out of here," I said.

The distinct sound of high heels clicking on the floor were followed by a shuffle. Two people were in the mayor's office.

"The only ways out are the stairs and elevator, and we have to pass by the mayor's office for both," Olivia said.

"Maybe the mayor will go into her office and shut the door?" I whispered close to Olivia's ear.

She clawed at my arm. "If we're caught, Uncle Callan is going to send me to boarding school."

"Okay." I patted her hand. "We'll find our way out." Even if it meant using another touch of the fairy dust.

We scurried forward hand-in-hand to crouch behind Brianna's desk chair.

"I will be paid in full. That was the agreement," a man's voice said.

"I'm doing the best I can," the mayor responded. "If I could get into my work laptop I could show you the email where I canceled your services well ahead of time. I should only have forfeited the deposit."

The sound of a click soon followed her words. The urge to get a better look at the man overwhelmed me, but I needed to focus on Olivia's safety first. I crawled to the edge of the desk and laid flat against the floor. From this angle I could the profile of a man, and he held a gun.

Fear froze me to the spot. I'd never seen a real gun before, but I knew they ended lives with a single trigger pull. How did I protect Olivia?

The man waved the gun toward the desk. "Give me what you have. I'm not leaving town until I get it all, and my patience is worn thin."

The man with the gun turned to the side a little

more and I realized it was the same man that had been arguing with the mayor in the alley. The nice guy, Vinnie. Lesson learned on people not being what they seem.

The mayor rifled through her desk drawers, and I scooted on my stomach back to Olivia. I made a gun symbol and her jaw dropped. We were in serious trouble.

I moved the rolling chair to the left and gently shoved her beneath the desk. I leaned in close. "Stay here no matter what happens."

She nodded and withdrew a cell phone from her pocket. The screen lit up and cast light on her face and reflected in her glasses. She mouthed, "I'm calling for help."

"I'll cause a distraction," I mouthed back and wiggled back to my spying position at the corner of the desk.

"The money was here, I swear it was," Mayor Caldwell's voice raised an octave in panic.

"I think you've been jerking me around this entire time," Vinnie said. "I'm going to kill you and your cheating husband and make it look like a murder-suicide. Free of charge."

Whoa. Dark. I'd have to use the remainder of my fairy dust on this devil in disguise.

"I wouldn't do that if I were you," I stepped out

into the light coming from the mayor's office.

Vinnie turned the gun on me. "What are *you* doing here?"

I needed to get into face-toss range. I had nothing going for me. Except the fake psychic thing.

"The raccoon told me you were here," I said and took a tentative half-step forward.

"The what now?" he asked.

Confusion. *Good.* "I can speak to animals, and this raccoon that lives in the dumpsters behind the alley told me you were here with a gun. He didn't know who else to tell."

His gun arm had slouched but he straightened it and stepped toward me looking outside the office. "Who did you tell?"

"No one. I came straight here," I assured him. I didn't want him searching around and finding Olivia under the desk.

He grumbled something under his breath.

"I'm sorry?" I put a hand up to my ear and took another big step forward.

He barely noticed how we'd become within arm's reach of one another. "I said I don't usually have to kill some many people at one time. This is very annoying."

"Why are you killing anyone at all? It seems to me that you could choose to kill no one." One more step and I couldn't miss.

"That's my job," he stated flatly and pointed the gun back at Mayor Caldwell. "I kill people for a living. And usually I get paid really well, unless someone tries to stiff me."

I needed his focus on me. "Couldn't you get another job?"

His shoulders slumped. "This is what I'm good at. Now, Juniper, you are a real nice girl and I'm sorry I have to kill you, but if you don't stop asking me questions, I'm going to do it sooner than later."

"Sure," I said, then tossed my entire bag of fairy dust in his face. "Bad luck!"

He coughed and sputtered and dropped to his knees. "It burns, holy mother of fire, it burns." Even though he clawed at his face with one hand, the gun remained in the other.

Mayor Caldwell, who'd remained silent throughout our exchange, screeched at me, "Get the gun from his hands before he shoots us!"

"Stand back!" A voice came from behind us. "Everyone down on the ground!"

I didn't know why I needed to get on the ground, but I did as the stern voice instructed. I touched my nose to the floor and waited.

Several pairs of men's shoes ran past my face. "Juniper?"

I turned my face to the side. "Callan?"

"Where's Olivia?"

"Under the desk." I stuck out my arm and pointed to Brianna's desk.

He rushed over and pulled her out. She fell into his arms and clung to him.

A body belonging to one of the pairs of men's shoes crouched down beside me. "You can stand up now, miss."

"I'm not sure I can." My body had turned to jelly the minute I knew we were no longer in immediate danger.

The man stuck a hand in my face, and I reached for it. He pulled me to my knees first and then to my feet.

The man with the scar.

"You," I said.

"Agent Steven Fisher, FBI," he introduced himself.

Callan had calmed Olivia and they approached us. "What's the FBI doing in Lilac Cove?"

"Chasing down a contract killer. One of your citizens was planning to turn in evidence yesterday morning that a contracted hit had been taken out by their significant other."

"You're John Bleaker's interview," I said, putting the time line together.

Agent Fisher eyed me with a hint of surprise in his expression. "I can't confirm any specific details in an ongoing investigation."

"Why were you following me around?" I asked.

"You showed up at the same time as some very interested things happened in this town. I didn't think it was a coincidence."

Officer Foster walked a handcuffed Vinnie past us. Tears streamed down the hit man's face. "If I'm blind, I'm going to sue you, Juniper."

"Fair enough," I said. I'd be gone in a couple of days and his suing wouldn't matter.

Chief Rayburn walked the mayor out of her office next. "Come on, Nicole. You have some questions to answer and we're going to search your office real good."

She cut her eyes to me. "I don't know whether to thank you or spit on you."

After she walked past, I turned to Olivia. "Are you okay?"

Callan stepped in front of her. "You don't get to talk to her. I don't completely understand what the two of you are doing here, but my niece never should have been in this building with you and a man with a gun." I opened my mouth to explain but he shook his head. "I need to get her home now."

"He's mad," Agent Fisher said. "I'll explain to

him that she went in after you even after I'm pretty sure you'd told her to go home."

"You were watching us?"

"Like I said. I was here to find a killer and I couldn't be sure who it was. As I'm sure you're well aware, appearances can be deceiving. It could've been you." He tucked his badge and identification into his back pants pocket. "Once I heard the call come over the scanner about a man with a gun, the pieces fell into place."

Me, a contract killer? I glanced down at what Olivia had described as my ninja outfit. Okay, I could maybe see how my actions could be taken as suspicious.

Another Lilac Cove police officer approached us, and Agent Fisher nodded to me. "We'll take this one's statement in the morning. Right now, I'd like to search the mayor's office."

"I don't have to stay?" I asked.

"Do you need someone to escort you home?"

"I can make it back on my own. I'd like to get back in before Mossy notices I'm gone."

Chapter Sixteen

The next morning Mossy opened Fairyland Flowers to a group of customers. I'd told her about the night's events, but not until after she'd had her morning cup of tea. She'd been unhappy with me but proud I'd stopped an evil man from hurting more people.

Emory stood at the head of the group of customers with Allondra not far behind.

I stifled a yawn and worked with Mossy to fill flower orders. It seemed that as soon as the mayor's integrity came under fire, the town realized that Mossy's should have never been questioned.

After Emory paid for her bundle of wildflowers, she pulled on my sleeve. "Come down to the café when you get a break. We have some news to share with you."

"I'll be down in a few." I looked forward to seeing what information I could exchange with the gossip club.

"Oh, go on now," Mossy said, leaning across the counter. "I'm used to running the shop on my own, and this isn't Walmart on a Black Friday."

I'd never been in the human world on Black Friday or inside a Walmart, but I didn't need to in order to understand her reference. I stood back and marveled at the way Mossy greeted her customers and filled their orders. I couldn't imagine her sitting on a throne and doling out fairy errands all day.

Emory, Allondra, and I walked down to the Corner Café and found Gladys waiting for us inside.

Allondra sniffed. "I didn't see you at the flower shop this morning."

"I told you on the phone that I didn't need fresh flowers this week. I'll get an order from Mossy next week for the church to make it up to her."

"Good enough," Allondra said. "We take care of our own in Lilac Cove."

They didn't need their hypocrisy pointed out to them, no matter how much I wanted to remind them that only yesterday they'd believed Mossy to be involved in John's death.

Gladys tapped her fingers on the table, the urge to talk making her lips twitch. Was she waiting on me? Give a little to get a little from this crowd.

"The mayor got arrested last night," I started the conversation for them.

For the first time since I'd met her, Gladys forced a huge smile. It changed her entire appearance. "Officer Foster was in early this morning getting coffee and luckily so was I after Emory called me last night as soon as she heard the call go out over the scanner."

Allondra leaned in and rolled her hands in a circular motion. "Get on with it."

"Not only did the mayor hire a hitman to take out her philandering husband, she must have found out that John was going to tell on her to the FBI. They found what they think is the murder weapon, his laptop, blank Fairyland Flowers invoices, and a stack of cash hidden in her office."

I remembered Agent Fisher telling me that ongoing investigation information had to be kept secret. "Should he have told you all that?"

"I have my ways of getting people to talk." She sat back, satisfaction radiating from her as we all soaked her words in.

Emory tsked. "That's quite bold of her to keep all that evidence right there in her office."

Allondra shoulder's shook with a humorless chuckle. "Criminals aren't smart. I watch those late-night drama reenactments on ID Discovery and the police always catch up with the crazies."

"Do you think they'll do one of those made for tv movies here?" Emory asked.

I sat back and toyed with the edge of the teacup in front of me. I should have felt something more like relief at the capture of John's murderer, but instead something didn't sit right in my gut. One thing I'd learned in the past few days is that nothing was uncomplicated when it came to humans and their actions. If Mayor Caldwell had been the one to falsify the receipts to steal the petty cash and had the cash in her office, why wouldn't she hand it over to Vinnie when he threatened her with the gun?

Allondra poured hot water in her cup and added a tea steeper. "The city council will need to hold special elections, and soon. We don't have a mayor or deputy mayor anymore."

Gladys nodded in agreement. "The mayor's crime spree took out a third of the mayor's office in one swoop."

"Well, I never." Emory pointed outside of the café.

Dr. Caldwell and Brianna walked hand-in-hand down the sidewalk.

"Brianna didn't waste any time, did she?" Gladys asked. "She'll have Dr. Fool Around divorced and remarried before Mayor Caldwell's trial begins."

"Those two deserve each other," Emory added.

Allondra placed a hand on her chest. "I just had the worst thought. What if they cancel the May Day Festival? I've so been looking forward to the pet psychic tent, Juniper."

In all the excitement I'd forgotten about faking a psychic talent. "Ladies, I have a confession to make."

Gladys narrowed her eyes at me. "We don't need any more confessions. We chose you for our tent and you're going to be there to talk to some dogs."

I nodded, deciding it was wise not to go against Gladys and her gossip club. "Of course I will."

I'd already faked being human for a couple of days, I guess I could fake talking to pets too.

Emory patted my hand. "I found the perfect outfit for you in the back of my closet. An old Halloween costume I'd worn in the 50s. I'll drop it off at Mossy's before tomorrow afternoon."

"Sounds fun," I said. It really did. I looked forward to spending my final night in Lilac Cove with my new friends.

We finished our tea and gossip and shortly after I returned to Fairyland Flowers to assist Mossy with customers for the rest of the day.

After she locked the door at six, she turned to me with a smile. "We haven't had a proper dinner since you've been here. And since I don't cook other than with a microwave, I've decided to take you out."

We headed toward her car and before we could get inside the clunky monster, a Lilac Cove police car pulled in beside it. Chief Rayburn exited. He came around the side of Mossy's car and gave her shoulder a gentle squeeze.

"Juniper, the mayor is asking to see you."

"What? Why?"

He glanced up and down the sidewalk to make sure no passersby were within earshot. "She's admitting to hiring the hitman and then canceling after she lost her nerve last minute, but she says she didn't kill John Bleaker. She thinks you can use your psychic abilities to prove her innocence."

Mossy shook her head hard, her silver hair whipping around her face. "Juniper has done enough. It's your job now, Greg, to finish this thing up."

"I really don't know what more I could do," I added.

"I thought as much but now I can go back and tell her you said no."

"Can I ask one question, Chief Rayburn?" I continued when he nodded. "How did John know about her plan to hire a hitman?"

"Now, keep this to yourself. She used her laptop to contact the man she hired. John somehow found it and planned to show to the FBI agent. Best we can figure, she killed him to get it back. She's denying all of it though."

Mossy wrapped an arm around my shoulder. "She's obviously a very troubled woman."

"She's grasping at straws now that she's caught," the chief agreed. "She's going to prison for a very long time. We're releasing John's remains to his family in a few days. They plan to have the funeral out of state."

Mossy dropped her arm and I could sense that she had some unfinished business with John.

Chief Rayburn headed to his car and gave a short wave goodbye.

"Still want to go out for dinner?" Mossy asked.

I noted she tried to add cheerfulness to her voice but failed.

"Actually, I'd prefer it you microwaved me something and we chatted about all the years we haven't been together."

She smiled. "Let's do that."

Chief Rayburn backed out his police cruiser and headed in the direction of the police station. Weird that the mayor thought that I could or would help her.

I followed Mossy through the shop and into her apartment. She removed the frozen waffles from her freezer. "This is all I have, I'm afraid."

"That's fine." I opened Pip's cage and he joined us at the table.

Mossy heated the waffles in the toaster and placed plates, forks, and a bottle of syrup on the table.

When she put the waffles on our plates and sat down opposite me, I took the opportunity to ask her questions that she'd been good at avoiding the past few days. "Why did you send John the flowers?"

She forked a piece of waffle into her mouth and chewed slowly.

I tore a piece of my waffle, handing it to Pip and waited.

She put her fork down. "I saw him in the park a few days ago. He looked troubled, and I always hated the way we'd ended our relationship. I didn't speak to him but I wish now that I had. Sending flowers was my way of saying hello, I guess."

"Why did your relationship end?" I pushed even though it wasn't my business.

"John snooped into everything and when you're a banished fairy, that snooping isn't a good thing. He found a small packet of fairy dust that I'd kept for emergencies and…"

A pink blush started on her chest.

"And?" I asked.

"He thought it was drugs and flushed it down the toilet."

I snorted a laugh and put my hand over my mouth. "Oh my. All that magic dust in the sewage system."

She nodded, a smile forming on her lips. "John had strong morals and most people don't know this but he dumped me on the spot. He gave me a few rehab pamphlets and suggested I get my life right."

"Ouch."

"Surprisingly, he didn't tell anyone."

"Is that why you were acting suspicious about his death and not wanting me to get involved?" I asked.

She picked up her fork and started eating again. "If I say yes, can we move on to another conversation? I'd really like to hear more about your best friend Iris and this captain of the guard that is courting you."

I still had many questions about Mossy's life after leaving the kingdom, but I respected her enough to back off. Pip nudged my hand, and I gave him another piece of waffle.

The rest of the evening we spent time as a reunited aunt and niece should, talking boyfriends and shoes and making promises we'd find a way to stay in touch when my time there ended.

After Mossy crawled into bed and the snoring began, I settled with Pip on the sofa. He settled near my shoulder and nuzzled my neck.

"Everything seems to have turned out happily ever after," I whispered to him. But the messy, complicated lives of humans seemed anything but that. At least I could go home knowing I'd done my best to clean up the mess I'd created.

Chapter Seventeen

The next morning, I regarded myself in Mossy's mirror. I looked ridiculous. Absurd, one could even say.

"Come out and let us see, my dear." Mossy called from the other side of the screen. She and Emory waited for me to show off my pet psychic costume.

I wore a thick black curly wig with a shiny scarf that had fake gold coins hanging on my forehead. A matching necklace with the fake gold coins stacked in rows hung from my neck. The white off the shoulders blouse sleeves ballooned all the way to my wrists. The long red skirt stopped above my ankles and I had three scarves in pink, yellow, and blue tied at my waist.

Gladys had stopped by to do my makeup and

she'd drawn thick black eyebrows that gave me a look of constant surprise. She'd set the look with bright red lipstick.

But the worst of the costume were the faux fairy wings Mossy had asked me to clip on my back. She'd insisted that if I were going to help the gossip club with their tent, I could at least assist with promoting her business by wearing the wings. I didn't connect the two and figured she only did it as a joke to see me squirm.

"Please don't let the fairy godparents be watching from the fountain," I whispered into the air.

I pulled the screen back and gave my audience a twirl. The wings bounced behind me. Emory clapped and Mossy let out a slow wolf whistle.

"Off to the festival," Emory said.

I left Pip's cage on the counter and gave him a scratch under the chin before securing the door. As much fun as it would be to have him in the tent with me, I didn't want any of the cats or dogs to scare him.

We walked out the front door and followed signs pointing toward the May Day Festival.

The streets around the town square had been marked off for the day and the majority of the vendors set up tents in the park. Mossy stayed behind to capture any customers that would browse the square shops before heading home. She promised she'd check in on me at some point.

I hoped that meant a rescue.

Gladys and Allondra waited for us beneath the tent, and I couldn't hide how impressed I was with the set up. They'd hung red sheets over the tent and had the door secured with velvet ribbons to create an entrance. Mini-lights were hung across the top. A painted sign standing by the entrance said *Pet Psychic, $5 to know your pet's thoughts.*

Inside there were two small tables draped in a white cloth, one with dog treats in a bowl and the other with a fake crystal ball. Allondra had put a picture of Killer inside the fake crystal ball. A larger table sat in the middle with a red tablecloth and two white chairs. Several dog beds were situated around the chairs.

Oh dear. This was serious. An ache started in the middle of my chest that I recognized to be a bout of anxiety. I hope I didn't let the gossip trio down.

"Our first customer," Allondra said and pushed me toward the chair. She pretended to adjust my head scarf as she whispered, "It's Molly Fergland's Chihuahua, Spanky, and he has abandonment issues since she's gone back to work."

A woman with short cropped hair came through

the entrance holding her dog who squirmed. He wore a thick knitted sweater and hassled with his tongue hanging out.

She sat down and I smiled at her. "How can I help you and Spanky today?"

"Poor Spanky hasn't been himself lately."

"Since you went back to work?" I offered.

Molly sat a little straighter. "Yes. I put this comfort sweater on him but he's been very lethargic."

I let Spanky sniff my fingers before giving him a soft rub on the head. I reached for a treat and when I offered it to him, he snatched it up. "When did you start putting this sweater on him?"

She fidgeted with the edge of her dog's collar. "The night before I started. He's been wearing it for two weeks."

"It's May and too hot for a dog in Florida to have on a sweater this thick. Take it off and put it in his bedding if you think he really needs it, but nobody wants to run around in this heat with something like that on. I'd be lethargic too."

She nodded her head.

Allondra stood behind her and rolled her hands for me to continue.

I touched my finger to the tip of his nose as if I could actually absorb his thoughts. "He's going to miss you no matter what. Give him extra cuddles in the evening when you're home and he'll eventually come around to the new routine."

Molly thanked me and began pulling the thick sweater off of Spanky before she'd made it out the door.

Allondra giggled. "One down and we already have a line of five or six customers waiting with their pets. The mysterious events of you popping into town unexpectedly and catching the mayor by talking to a raccoon will make certain that we win *Most Donations Received* this year."

I blew a hard breath and it lifted one of the fake coins off of my forehead.

Emory leaned in the tent. "Brianna and her poodle B.B. are next."

Allondra rolled her eyes. "That poor dog needs a different owner. That'd be the best advice you can give her."

"Just because she had an affair with the mayor's husband?"

"No, because I hear her yelling at the poor dog all the time."

Emory led Brianna and B.B. to the table. B.B. sank down on a pet bed and Brianna snatched the harness with a jerk. "Sit up, B.B., you lazy animal." She gave me an apologetic shrug. "She's supposed to be a purebred."

"Maybe she just wants to be a dog." I grabbed two treats from the bowl and tossed them to her. B.B. gobbled them up and sniffed the air searching out more.

Brianna ignored my comment. "All I need to know is why she's scared of water."

Was Brianna planning a cruise so soon after the mayor's arrest?

She held up her cell phone. "Can I take a selfie with you and B.B.?"

"I don't think so," I said.

At the same time Allondra answered, "Pictures cost extra."

Brianna yanked the harness and pulled B.B. over to sit next to me. I let her sniff my hands and I rubbed the top of her fluffy head. She pushed against my hand as if soaking up the much-needed affection. Poor dog. Why have a pet if you didn't want to give it all the love in the world?

Brianna pushed her face close to mine and used her thumb to find her camera. As she switched to the right screen, my eye caught a picture. It was the same boat that had been on her screensaver at the mayor's office. The same boat that had been on the screen saver on the computer on John's coffee table. The one with the swirly *B*.

Weird that their laptops had the same screensaver and she used it for her phone too. But that wasn't right. The laptop on John's coffee table was supposed to be the mayor's that he'd taken from the office. How had that laptop made it back to the mayor's office and onto Brianna's desk?

Brianna took the picture of us and studied it for a few seconds. "I like the way you're looking over at me in awe. Makes me look important."

I didn't know how to put together what I knew, and as far as motive, means, and opportunity, the mayor did have the three stacked against her. Except, wasn't Brianna the mayor's alibi? Had Brianna lied for the mayor and in doing so lied for herself? Would the police question that again?

Brianna sat opposite me and gestured to B.B. "We're ready. What's she saying about me?"

I toyed with my bottom lip. How could I use B.B. to get answers from Brianna? "B.B. misses your old boyfriend."

Brianna rolled her eyes. "John did have a soft spot for her. He spoiled her really. But your new daddy is going to buy us a great big house far away from here."

She'd switched her voice to baby talk when she spoke to B.B. about Dr. Caldwell.

The mention of John hadn't unnerved her.

Time to take a bold move. I touched my finger to B.B.'s nose. "B.B. also says that she knows what really happened to John and she's not happy about it."

This bait caught a reaction. Brianna stood and snatched B.B.'s harness, pulling her back. B.B. whined with the force of it.

"I don't know what you're trying to do, you big phony, but this is the second time I've had to warn you to mind your own business." Her face tightened with a hint of quiet rage. "You won't get a third."

She pushed past Allondra and dragged B.B. behind her.

"What happened there?" Allondra asked.

Brianna's motive hit me like I'd hit Vinnie in the face with the fairy dust. With the mayor out of the way she had Dr. Caldwell all to herself. But that didn't make sense.

Did she find out that John intended to talk to the FBI about the mayor? I shook my head. The mayor would be out of the way and she'd still have Dr. Caldwell anyway. That didn't give her a reason to kill John. What would he know about Brianna that would be worth killing for?

"Hon, you're starting to worry me," Allondra said.

"Does Brianna own a sailboat?" I asked.

Emory poked her head in and sniffed. "She doesn't have the money for that. She'd have to rob somebody blind."

"But what if she did? Where would she keep it?" I stood up and took the wig and scarf off. "The sailboat, I mean."

"There's a boat dock not far from the beach," Allondra said. "There are a handful of boats in the boat slips."

"What's the fastest way to get to the boat dock?" All the clues were floating around in my head, but I needed to see the boat to know if I was right before I called Chief Rayburn.

"What about our booth?" Gladys came into the tent.

Emory shushed her. "She's using her psychic stuff right now. We'll worry about the booth later. Follow your instincts, girl."

I rushed out of the tent and the first person I ran into was Callan. He gave me a frown. "Olivia is missing the festival because of you."

I grabbed his shoulders. "I know and I'm really sorry, but right now I need to get to the boat dock."

"I walked to the square. My truck is at home." He pulled my hands away from him. "What's wrong?"

"I can't right now," I said and ran away from

him toward Fairyland Flowers. If Brianna planned to sail away on her boat before I could prove she was involved, the police might not catch her.

I needed a car. Mossy's was parked outside the square in case she needed it before they removed all the barricades. She'd put the keys above the visor telling me that in the twenty years she'd owned it no one had ever tried to steal it.

The beast loomed in front of me like a dragon needing to be tamed. Even with the magic to know things in the human world, driving a car meant putting myself and others in danger if I got even one step wrong.

But my need to get answers surpassed that. I slid into the driver's seat and cringed at the hot vinyl that I could feel through the thin fabric of the skirt. I put the keys into the ignition and cranked it. The engine turned over with a growl.

I still didn't know my way to the dock.

The driver's door opened and Callan leaned down. "Emory told me they think you're having a psychic episode. I think psychotic might be the right word, but I don't want you stumbling into another scene like with the mayor and the hitman."

"Can you get me to the closest boat dock near the beach? I can explain everything from there." At least I could try.

"Scoot," he said.

I crawled across the bench seat to the passenger's side.

Callan guided the car onto the road and followed the signs that pointed toward the beach and dock.

"You have to tell me something before we get there," he said.

"My deductions were all wrong," I started. "Sherlock would not be impressed. I assumed John's death to be about what he knew about the mayor but it's about money."

"How do you mean?" Callan pulled into a small parking lot in front of a long wooden walkway that led to a scattering of different sized boats parked in boat slips. At the end, a white sailboat with a swirly *B* swayed gently in the water.

"If that sailboat belongs to who I think it belongs to, then I think I know who stole John's inheritance money and all the petty cash." I climbed out of the car but leaned back in to finish. "I think Brianna killed John because he accidently took her laptop from the mayor's office and she thought he knew about her stealing money. But he didn't yet. He only knew about the mayor's plans to kill her husband."

"You can prove this?" He asked exiting the car and joining me on the path to the boat docks. "If so, proper police procedure needs to be followed for chain of evidence. We can't break and enter and find something that could be thrown out of court later for being mishandled."

"I just need to see something first." I couldn't connect it exactly in my head but I knew that the laptop Brianna had in the office was the same one that I'd seen on John's coffee table. She'd told the mayor that John had all their laptops for updates. What if John had taken the wrong laptop from the office when he'd meant to take the mayor's? His laptop had never really been missing at all. *There has to be a clue that makes it all fit on the boat.* My instincts were sure of it.

We walked out onto the dock and came up to the sailboat. I called out, "Anyone there?"

Callan crossed his arms. "We shouldn't."

"No, you really should," said a voice from behind us.

Brianna checked to the left and right before fully extending her arm and showing her gun. B.B. stood at her side and whimpered.

Did everyone have a gun? "How did you know we were coming here?"

"I didn't." She dropped the leash in her other hand and it fell to the dock. "I came straight here from the festival to force B.B. to get over her fear of water, but she wouldn't get out of the car. Then I saw the two of you pull into the parking lot and realized that B.B. had told you what happened to John."

"She really didn't," I said, a little frustrated at how easily the people of Lilac Cove believed I had a psychic ability.

"Get on the boat. Both of you," she said. "I told you there wouldn't be a final warning, Juniper. I'm doing this town a favor by getting rid of you. Out of every nosy person in Lilac Cove, you are the worst in that you won't let things go."

I stepped over the side and onto the boat. "My best friend Iris says that I have that problem too."

"Found out by a pet psychic." She waited for Callan to get on the boat before she unloosed the rope attached to the metal cleat. "I should have stayed away from that stupid festival." She turned a glare on B.B. "This is your fault."

"I'm not really a pet psychic," I said wanting to put an end to that lie. I didn't want her to hurt B.B. either.

"There's no other way you could have known all the things you know." She left B.B. on the pier and stepped over the railing onto the sailboat. "But they will die with you at the bottom of the ocean. I'll start a quick rumor that you and the dispatch guy have run off together. The gossip hags will love that."

Callan glanced at me and back at Brianna. "I don't even know her. Why would I run off with her?"

"The people in that town will believe anything now that Mayor Caldwell has tried to have my sweetie bumped off. And as soon as William cleans out his shared bank account, we'll be sailing this boat into the sunset."

Another dose of fairy dust would have been real nice right about now.

"Daddy, if you're watching, I could use some help," I called out into the air.

"You are as weird as your aunt," Brianna said and shook her head.

I'd known that probably wouldn't work. Dad couldn't risk exposing the fairy godparent world to save me. At least I'd tried.

"How are you going to sail us out to the ocean with a gun in your hand?" Callan asked.

I knew he stalled for time. Good idea.

"I could work this boat with my feet," Brianna answered.

"Really?" I asked and moved close to the edge of the boat to peer over the side into the water. "Show me."

She moved close to me and put the gun near my

stomach. "I'm going to shoot you first."

I needed to stall for more time like Callan. "I need to know I'm right about how things happened."

"I don't owe you anything. It's not like you're going to have the chance to tell anyone."

"But you're the one who stole the petty cash right and set up my aunt? And you stole John's inheritance money too? That's how you can afford this sailboat." I flickered my eyes toward the boat dock. What were the chances that someone would come down to look at the boats with the festival going on and see us? "Were you born awful or did something happen to make you this way?"

She lowered the gun as if my question had struck a sensitive nerve. "I'm awful? Mayor Caldwell was going to kill William. John couldn't mind his own business to save his life— *literally*! I'm surrounded by awful. At least now I'll live the life I've always deserved."

From my peripheral vision I could see Callan edging backwards toward the front of the boat. I had to give him time to get out of her line of fire.

I couldn't let Callan die and leave Olivia without anyone to raise her. I'd thought I could walk into the human world and fix the mess I'd made but I'd only made it worse minute by minute. My dad had been right. If I'd left things alone then even if it had taken months, the police would have had a better chance of seeing through Brianna's lies.

"One last question. Why did you hit John with a brick?" I asked. "He didn't even know about the theft."

"I didn't know that. I only used my key to sneak in and when I got to his living room he was on the phone with the police. My laptop was open on the coffee table. How was I supposed to know he'd meant to take the mayor's laptop instead? He could have ruined everything."

And now I was out of options. Except for one. At least one of the Sherlock Holmes stories I read gave me a real solution. The one where Sherlock goes over the edge of a cliff to take down his nemesis. I prayed that with all the magical knowledge bestowed upon me to know what to do in the human world, swimming would also be one of them. As soon as Brianna noticed Callan moving and turned the gun away from my stomach, I grabbed her by the arms and pulled her with me over the side.

We hit the water in a tangle of arms and legs. I held my breath and flailed, slapping my way to the top. Brianna hadn't dropped the gun and she held it above her head.

B.B. barked and barked and with a graceful leap, jumped into the water and paddled her way to us. As soon as she reached Brianna, she bit her hard on the shoulder.

Brianna screamed and the gun fell from her hand.

I sputtered and drank a mouthful of saltwater. My throat stung and I yelled to Callan who'd watched us from the sailboat. "I don't think I can swim."

He jumped over the side and grabbed me under the arms. The four of us swam to a ladder at the end of the dock. I held on to the side while Callan pushed B.B. onto the wooden walkway.

Brianna scrambled up the ladder and broke into a run toward the cars. She held a hand over her bleeding shoulder.

Callan climbed up first and then extended a hand to me. "That was brave and stupid at the same time."

I sat on the ground and coughed, my chest and throat hurting.

B.B. licked my face.

I lifted an arm and pointed to the parking lot. "What do we do about her?"

Callan shook his head. He pulled his phone out of pocket. "Good thing I sprung for the new waterproof cell phone."

He stepped away and told someone on the other side what had happened and to be on the lookout for Brianna, who'd probably need stitches on her shoulder.

I patted B.B.'s white curly fur on the top of her head, now wet and dripping water. "I knew you weren't scared of water. You just didn't like her."

Callan hung up the phone and helped me to standing, my fake wings bouncing behind me. He shook his head. "Are you always followed around by this much bad luck?"

My shoulders shook as I chuckled. "I'm meant to bring good luck if you want to know the truth."

The person who'd gotten the worst of the luck had been John Bleaker.

Sirens blasted in the distance.

Callan squeezed my hands before letting them go. "I don't think Brianna will make it very far with Officer Quick on her trail."

"Thanks for believing in me," I said.

"If you aren't a psychic then how did you know?"

I couldn't tell him the truth even if I wanted to. And I wanted to. I pushed wet hair out of my face. "Would you believe me if I said all my detective skills come from reading Sherlock Holmes?"

"I'm still not okay with Olivia following you into the mayor's office, so don't be surprised if I don't ask you out for coffee any time soon." He turned his back to me and headed toward Mossy's car, seeming to let the question of how I'd figured out Brianna to be the murderer go for now.

I trudged forward in the soaked costume, the skirt dripping water onto the pier. It didn't matter about the coffee date, I told myself. Amaranth would be here for me tomorrow anyway. I smiled despite the scary turn of events. I'd solved John's murder and he'd get justice. All without my magic wand. And only the tiniest smidge of fairy dust.

Chapter Eighteen

Mossy chose not to be there when Amaranth came to collect me, so we said our goodbyes in the main flower shop. My father hadn't set a designated meeting place for my return to Juniper Springs, so I stood alone in the middle of my aunt's one-bedroom apartment. Waiting. If Dad was still watching me through the fountain, he'd know where to send his captain of the guard.

Officer Foster had been the one to track down and arrest Brianna. Dr. Caldwell had denied any involvement in her plans according to the information Chief Rayburn passed along to Mossy.

Callan had chosen to forgive me enough to allow Olivia to say goodbye. She'd given me a hug and apologized for causing so much trouble. I'd whispered in her ear that I thought her to be just as good a detective as Sherlock Holmes. Then I asked her to take good care of B.B. I'm pretty sure giving Olivia a dog put me right back on Callan's bad luck list. But he'd given me a wink and goodbye wave before they'd turned away.

Two of the three gossip club members had also stopped by to wish me well. Gladys had yet to forgive me for letting another tent win the *Most Donations Received* plaque at the festival but Emory and Allondra said she'd get over it with time.

Pip climbed the back of my dress and hung onto my shoulder. I couldn't leave my new friend behind. "Pip, Pip. Hungry."

"As soon as we get to Juniper Springs, I'll have Dad restore your ability to say complete sentences."

He flicked his tail in response.

I turned in a slow circle, unsure how I felt about going home. A heaviness rested on my shoulders, as if I had unfinished business.

In a glamorous poof of pink sparkles, my mother appeared. She glanced around and immediately wrinkled her nose. "Interesting."

Pip bounded off my shoulder and ran toward his cage.

I couldn't help my grin even though I chastised her. "Don't be a snob, Mom."

She opened her arms wide and I rushed into

them.

"How I've missed you these past few days," she said.

"I missed you too."

She held on for a few beats more before pushing me away and searching my face. "You appear less fragile than before."

"I've never been fragile," I said.

"That's how your father and I see you. Our little girl trying too hard to fly from the nest." She peeked around me. "Where's your aunt?"

"She didn't want to be here." I gestured over my shoulder to the flower shop. "I think seeing real fairies pop in and out of her apartment brings up old feelings. Not so good ones."

"I can imagine." She led me to the sofa and we sat facing each other.

"Why didn't you tell me Aunt Mossy gave up the throne?"

"It's a sore subject with your father. He didn't want to be king. He liked being a prince who could get away with coming and going as he pleased." She wiggled her perfectly manicured eyebrows at me. "Reminds me of you."

"You would never guess. He shoulders the responsibility so well." I ducked my head. "How angry is he?"

Her smile never faltered. "That you put your life in danger twice? Very. That you asserted your independence? He's slowly getting over it. We're very impressed with you."

I drew an imaginary circle on the couch with my finger. "Well…I'm ready to go back now. Can I have my wand?"

"Not just yet."

"What? Why not?"

"Your father and I have decided that your argument about being too sheltered is valid. We're going to do what some human parents do and consider this sending you abroad for a semester. Or something similar." She cut her hand through the air as if she didn't care if she got the reference correct.

"You want me to stay in Lilac Cove?"

"Only through the remainder of summer and into fall. We'll expect you home before Christmas. And absolutely no more of this inserting yourself into crime solving."

I shrugged, trying to hide my delight at sticking around. "What are the chances of that happening again?"

She withdrew her wand and waved it in the air as plastic cards and a couple of keys began poofing into existence and dropping to the floor. Pip came away from his cage and picked at the edge of one of the cards.

"I've won one major argument against your father. You are royalty, and shall live as such. Here is the key to your cottage near the beach, the keys to your convertible should you choose to learn to drive, your wallet full of credit cards and a bank account in your name."

"Huh?"

"Pip, Pip?" Pip said.

"We're fairy godparents, sweetie. We can be as wealthy as we want in the human world." She picked up the wallet from the floor and picked out a card. "This is your identification card. It allows you to drive."

I read the name out loud. "Juniper F. Airie?"

Her tinkle of a laugh filled the room. "I came up with that one myself."

"I'm shocked."

She stood and unfurled her wings. "Get this human world stuff out of your system. Then come home and focus on the important things."

I had to admit the idea of sticking around Lilac Cove filled me with an anticipation I hadn't expected. The humans were complicated beings and understanding them would only benefit the way we handled our fairy errands.

"One more thing," I said and pointed to Pip.

"Do you really need a talking squirrel, Juniper?" she asked.

"Please?"

She tapped his head with her wand three times. "Speak only to Juniper."

"Thank you." I stood and hugged her again whispering against her shoulder, "Are you sure I can't keep a little fairy dust on hand for emergencies too?"

"Check your underwear drawer when you get to the cottage," she whispered.

We broke apart. "Tell Dad I love him."

"He knows." She tapped her wand on top of her head and said, "Home."

With a poof, she vanished.

I sorted through the materials on the floor thinking of all the good I could do in the amount of time I'd been given.

Pip hopped around me. "What should we do first?"

I held up the keys to my cottage. "Watch out human world, here we come."

ABOUT THE AUTHOR

K.M. Waller aka Kizzie Waller lives in Florida with her husband, two kids, and their popcorn-loving hermit crab. When she's not reading, writing, or chasing her kids around the house, she loves to binge television dramas and mysteries.

If you ever see her in person, feel free to ask if she believes in fairies and witches and all things that go bump in the night.

MORE FROM THE AUTHOR

The Lost Souls ParaAgency Series: (Romantic paranormal mysteries)

Lost Souls ParaAgency and the Three Witches of Burberry

Lost Souls ParaAgency and the Ghostly Reunion

Lost Souls ParaAgency and the Illusion of a Vampire

Lost Souls ParaAgency and the Mysterious Bag of Bones

Come All Ye Witches (A LSP/Bad Witch Mystery Crossover)

Lost Souls ParaAgency and the Creature of White Oak Swamp

Bad Witch Takes a Case: A Bad Witch Mystery

Bad Witch Makes a Blunder: A Bad Witch Mystery

A Witch in Time paranormal mystery series: (Can be read as a standalone but a lot more fun if you read all the books in the series, each written by a different author)

Right Time Wrong Witch: A Witch in Time Mystery

Never Enough Time: A Witch in Time Mystery

Contemporary Mysteries:

Seven Lives to Kill: A Cat Sanctuary Cozy Mystery

Mourning Express: A Drop Dead Famous Cozy Mystery